The Struggling Cartoonist

A Cartoonyville Adventure!

The Struggling Cartoonist
What Lurked in the Linen Closet

Written and Illustrated by
Professor Mark Stephen Smith

Mountain Arbor
Press an Imprint of BookLogix
Alpharetta, GA

ISBN: 978-1-63183-959-7 - Paperback
eISBN: 978-1-63183-960-3 - ePub
eISBN: 978-1-63183-961-0 - mobi

Library of Congress Control Number: 2020925153

Printed in the United States of America   1 2 3 0 2 0

∞ This paper meets the requirements of ANSI/NISO Z39.48-1992 (Permanence of Paper)

*This book is dedicated to my dear wife and best
friend of a lifetime. (Thanks for having patience
with the studio clutter that led to this book.)*

Once you get people laughing, they're listening and you can tell them almost anything.
—Herbert Gardner

It takes a heap of sense to write good nonsense.
—Mark Twain

Contents

Preface

Mark: My Words

Being a Mini-Biography up to the Creation of Cartoonyville

Much like the self-styled protagonist, the semi-fictional Prof. Mark Toonery of the following story, my own journey to animation was a reluctant one.

Although I always drew, I don't recall ever seriously considering that I could make a living as a professional artist. I do, however, remember wanting to be a writer at an early age, having written my first unpublished "book" (of many), *Super-Snooper Detective Agency*, around age eleven. This was most likely written as a response to my favorite teen detectives, The Three Investigators, introduced to me by my favorite homeroom teacher in fifth grade.

Like most American kids, I watched cartoons well into my teen years, probably beyond most. Saturday morning cartoons were a treat, as were the few Tex Avery cartoons peppered among the local after-school broadcasts of *Tom and Jerry*, and the occasional CBS special (usually *It's the Great Pumpkin, Charlie Brown*, still one of my personal favorites for obvious reasons—yes, Halloween *is* actually my birthday).

Growing up "in the middle of the woods," as I often say—not in a log cabin, but in a modest brick home (my dad and uncle built it on land granted from my grandparents)—there was little to do in our hometown on the summers and weekends apart from fishing, hiking, or boating on the nearby lakes and rivers of rural Alabama. So, I learned what is sadly approaching an outdated art form in the digital age: the fine art of learning to entertain myself.

I learned to draw at an early age, as outlined briefly in my other book, *The Art of Flash Animation: Creative Cartooning*. And, perhaps curiously, at age sixteen I showed some of my Stephen King–wannabe and J.R.R. Tolkien-inspired fantasy characters to my Sunday school teacher, an attractive ranch owner in her mid-twenties. After examining a sampler of my short stories, she said to me, "Have you ever thought about writing for animation?"

My immortal reply to her that followed: "Animation? Animation is for *children*." This statement was soon to be turned upon me forevermore.

The story of Cartoonyville goes back to around September of 2012, when I was still working as an adjunct instructor for Westwood College. Westwood was what you'd probably call a technical college, based in Denver, but I had found my way there via the Atlanta campus. Their position "across the street" from Cartoon Network[1][*] was an added bonus for me,

---

[*] Technically, the main Turner campus that housed the Cartoon Network and Boomerang offices was across the freeway from the Westwood Building on Spring Street, but their Adult Swim offices were literally a walk across the corner.

as their various animators and directors would come over on Thursday nights for figure-drawing sessions in our downstairs "assembly room."

I had pitched a couple of shows to their previous Vice President of Original Programming Linda Simensky, but needless to say, for one reason or another, I missed their "target audience" of eleven to fourteen. My characters were either "too cute" or "too clean," and frankly, I had no interest in the shows that soon made their way onto the aptly named Adult Swim.

I wanted to make cartoons adults can enjoy *alongside* their kids.

Much like my namesake in the following story, *Who Framed Roger Rabbit* was my inspiration for an animated career. Roger Rabbit's curvy wife, Jessica Rabbit, quickly convinced me that animation wasn't "just for kids." And although the feature film proved animation is still viable entertainment for adults and kids alike, I don't think it necessarily has to be "adults only," either.

Oddly enough, though, my inspiration for Cartoonyville came from the *opposite* direction of the street.

Since the Subway half a block down had long since closed, the only place to get a quick meal (aside from a rather pricey lunch counter downstairs) was a block in the opposite direction to Sonic, where I could get a cheap cheeseburger for a dollar and some fries that were a little too spicy for my preference.

On this particular day, as I walked toward my

lunch-break destination, I couldn't help noticing a white van unloading lights into the building across from us. *Those are video lights*, I thought to myself. *And where there are video lights, there is video production*, I concluded.

After fetching my "cheapburger" and fries, I looked up the name of the company online, and found they were an Interfaith Broadcasting station. My initial idea was to offer some animated video promos for their station, and I called to make an appointment to discuss just that. They politely agreed, and an idea for a promo popped into my head that I would work on. However, as often happens when you least expect it . . . my creative brain juices started flowing, and quickly out of control.

Early the next morning, perhaps, I got an idea for a TV show. I could mix live-action, animation, *and* puppetry in a way that I'd seen nowhere else. Well, the closest I'd seen was in what I considered as close to perfection in modern family entertainment for literally all ages—*Pee-wee's Playhouse.*

Paul Reubens, in my opinion, is the latest in a long line of entertainment geniuses that I equate with Charlie Chaplin, Jim Henson, and Walter Lantz (the *other* famous Walt of animation, creator of Woody Woodpecker). And I should note (for reasons that become obvious later), especially in the latter two cases, part of their creative genius was that they owned *completely* their creative properties and related characters.

I quickly cobbled together a rough cut called an *animatic*. In animation, that just means you take storyboards (preferably in color) and time them out to a soundtrack. (I describe it to my clients as an "on-screen comic book with a soundtrack.") I called it *The Cartoonyville Studio Show*, in which a live-action professor of animation (yours truly) presided over a cartoon-themed amusement park, but instead of college students wearing sweaty character suits, this park actually was the residence of living cartoon characters, peppered with a few puppet characters to ease the strains surely our inevitably low budget could manage.

In the show, I would demonstrate to kids how to draw their own cartoons and comics, as well as make their own flipbooks and stop-motion animation. I took a graduate course at nearby SCAD from a wonderful instructor who insisted we call her "Prof. Becky," as her last name was tricky to pronounce. (This naturally led me to adopting my own screen name as "Prof. Mark.")

The producer I met with called their video director in to watch my presentation. I pushed the button to start my demo DVD, and they were both instantly impressed . . . and confused. "That's a great idea for a show," they said, "but we thought you were just going to show us a demo for some promo ideas you had."

Nevertheless, they liked the idea, and I soon recruited my Westwood students to help me with the pilot episode. Soon we were shooting greenscreen sequences of myself interacting with the cartoon characters in the animated theme park of Cartoonyville, notably Deadbeat Skunk and Thurman Q. Porcupine from my unpublished *Bigfoot Country* comic strip.

What at first seemed like a somewhat generous budget offer for a locally produced kids show would soon reveal itself to be woefully inadequate once we actually delivered the broadcast-ready episode. This became slowly but painfully obvious, especially as it took me nine months, working part time, to composite all the live-action elements, animation, and puppetry together.

One of my earlier thoughts during the concept phase was, *Why not combine 2D animation, puppetry, and live action in a cartoon environment? It's never been done before to my knowledge, so why hasn't anyone else tried this with all the digital tools we have in the Adobe Creative Suite (now Creative Cloud)?*

Nine months of unpaid, part-time production on one half-hour, *unaired* pilot episode.

That's why *not*, buster.

Because I had produced this episode "on spec" (without a contract or any money down), that meant they would provide me a contract *upon delivery* of the pilot episode. So, when I finally did approach them with the broadcast-ready DVD, that was my first opportunity to read over the contract. It was hardly the fearsome situation of the infamous Walt Disney–Charles Mintz meeting (expertly showcased in the film *Walt Before Mickey*), but there was a clause I was rather uncomfortable with . . .

Terribly uncomfortable with.

They wanted partial "ownership" of the characters appearing in the show, so to speak (which would include appearances in any other subsequent shows), and would receive royalties on related character merchandise. Something like that.

Like Walt Disney at his "Mintz meeting," when seemingly backed into a corner, I briefly considered their offer. I even had them put in an addendum about removing the Prof. Mark character from that royalty clause, which they obliged.

But in the end, just under one grand for all this work and allowing "outsiders" partial ownership of my characters was *not* what I wanted. Not when I had read about other animation pioneers like Ralph Bakshi, Jim Henson (yes, he did cartoons for *Sesame Street*, too), and Walter Lantz who owned their characters.

I respectfully declined their offer, we parted on amicable terms, and I had a much bigger challenge on my hands.

Now, I had to figure out what to *do* with this Cartoonyville idea.

I did discover another station in town, People TV, a public access station, that was happy to broadcast the episode. But sadly, public access doesn't pay. At least, not directly. Jim Henson became a millionaire licensing his characters on *Sesame Street*, but I didn't have that widespread an audience. At least not yet.

I hit upon the idea of *Cartoonyville Comics* for Free Comic Book Day, the first Saturday of every May. Although I didn't get "paid," I did somehow manage to sell ad space to some of my existing animation clients (not to mention Westwood College) that at least paid for my printing costs.

It was a start . . .

Around this time, I started wondering how "Prof. Mark" actually met these characters. I produced an animated short about how they were sharing a two-bedroom apartment with Prof. Mark and his wife, before they moved to this "temporarily fictional" theme park for living cartoons. But I needed to go back further. I wanted more of an origin story to introduce them all, and I decided that for whatever reason, they popped out of his sketchbook late one night.

So, here we are!

The reader will also note that from here on, most of the obvious names of my early influences have been changed to protect the legal integrity of the innocent (or in this case, at least, *me*). In writing my previous book, I had thought to include some artwork owned by a certain mouse-eared corporation, notably that of a certain bow-tied rabbit. (I bought an actual production drawing of *that* rabbit from the film, as a gift to myself from the advance check on the first book.) As you can guess, watching his first movie-screen appearance influenced me to this crazy career choice.

"Animation—*that's* what I wanna do for a living!"

However, upon advice from the editor of that book, I opted out of the "Mouse House's" participation. Because, as he suspected, they wanted roughly fifty bucks for every illustration. And my editor's caution was quickly justified, as the book was indeed published in several languages. (That would have added up, as much to my surprise, my few fan letters arrived from places as widespread as India, Germany, and Korea!)

However, I did keep one name of a true-life inspiration intact, that of Forrest J. Ackerman, publisher of *Famous Monsters* magazine, based upon a true-life meeting (if memory serves) in the hallways of the 1992 Atlanta Fantasy Fair.

But you'll read about that soon enough.

PROLOGUE:
Animation!

Young Mark Toonery, a slender theater student with a scruffy teenager's moustache, and his friend Danny, along with their two friends Rhonda and Angela, approached a movie theater in Birmingham, Alabama. Their high-school graduation had completed the week before, and the graduates had just a few days before their respective college plans would separate them.

Each had their different ideas of what they wanted to do: Danny in business, Angela and Rhonda in teaching and fashion design . . . but Mark was certain of his career. Having written a successful high-school play in their small community just an hour away, he had enrolled as a drama major, thinking he was destined to be a playwright.

His idea was about to drastically change that very evening.

With very little to do in their hometown, besides a small duplex cinema that was only open during the summer, Mark and his friends had always resorted to their own means of amusement during breaks. He and his friend Craig had performed puppet shows for their church Halloween carnivals, he had written an unpublished series of fantasy-adventure novels, and of course, he had always drawn. He started drawing cartoons like most kids, then mythical monsters to illustrate his stories, but what future was there in that? How could anyone possibly earn money *drawing* for a living? At least, that was the mindset in a small Alabama community like his, where the local movie theater couldn't even afford to support itself more than a few months at a time.

At least the turnout for his play had seemed successful enough to convince him of a possible career as a playwright, so he was set to begin as a theater major in Montevallo, less than half an hour's drive from both his home and Birmingham. Having lived his entire life comfortably in a small town, there seemed to be little need to drive any farther.

After purchasing their tickets, the two girls seated themselves on either side of their dates, with Danny and Mark sitting in the middle. Young Mark leaned over to his friend Danny, looking bored.

"Yeah, Danny, I like Demi Moone and all, but why this movie?" Mark asked with a sigh. "What's this *Seventh Sun* supposed to even be about? Some disaster film? Ugh . . ."

Danny grinned mischievously and winked at Mark. "You like brunettes! But hey, think about the rating, buddy—the rating! I did us a favor."

"She's *expecting*, Danny. Well . . . not exactly my idea of—"

The lights went down, and the previews began. Danny lowered his voice and continued with a chuckle, "Never mind, Mark. Just try to enjoy the previews."

"Oh, yeah. The previews. Whee!" Mark uttered a quick scoff. "Sure, pal."

With a long, exaggerated twang, a cartoony logo exploded onto the screen. *A Buffoon Cartoon! Starring Baby Melville and Jeremy Jackalope,* Mark read.

"See, look! A cartoon!" Danny said, lightly punching Mark's shoulder. "You told me you used to love cartoons."

"Cartoons?" Mark scoffed yet again. "Cartoons are for *children.*"

"This is coming from a guy who's done puppet shows for ten years?" Danny chuckled.

"Hey, my singing plant puppet won us second place in the talent show with that skit from *Little Shop of Heebie-Jeebies*! Besides," Mark added with another sigh, "I didn't think they showed cartoons before movies anymore. So, what is this, the 1960s?"

They watched onscreen as Jeremy Jackalope, a stuttering jackrabbit with antlers and denim overalls, walked through a park in a stroller with his passenger, Baby Melville, a sickeningly sweet toddler.

"C'mon, Baby Melville. Your mother will sk-sk-skin me alive if I let you get in trouble," Jeremy Jackalope gulped. "Again . . ."

While Jeremy was so distracted, he didn't watch where he was going and tripped into the park fountain with a noisy splash. Gurgling, the jackalope struggled to stand up, spouting a mouthful of water into the air. He wiped his eyes dry and noticed Baby Melville trapped inside a popcorn vendor's glass popper, clapping his pudgy hands in glee. Jeremy did a wild take in response, his eyes bugging out like a pair of extended dinner plates. "Yaaah!"

Young Mark leaned forward in his seat, keenly interested. "Wow, look how *smoothly* they move. They haven't made cartoons like this in thirty years ... forty!"

"Yeah," Danny agreed, laughing, almost dropping his popcorn. "Whoa-ho-ho!"

"Cut, you imbecile, cut!" exclaimed a voice on the movie screen.

All eight of the teens' eyes almost bugged out of their heads at what happened next. Suddenly, a live-action director stepped onto the cartoon set. Jeremy Jackalope shrunk back as he prepared for an onslaught of scolding from his boss.

"Jeremy Jackalope, what's wrong with you?" shouted the director. "Didn't you read the script? Good grief, you've gotta be the most overpaid cartoon actor in Hollywood! Ohhh, my achin' ulcer ..."

"Take one cartoon jackalope," said the unseen narrator as a montage of animated scenes began, "a detective down on his luck, and one sultry cartoon femme fatale, and you've got the biggest hit of this summer's film scene—*Who Drew Jeremy Jackalope?*"

"Well, look at that!" said Danny. "It was just a *preview* for a movie. Wow, mixing animation and live action? That's better than anything from *Barry Moppins*."

"Mixing animation and live action . . . wow," said Mark, realizing that somehow, this moment was drastically changing the course of his future.

"Animation, yeah . . . *animation*! That's what I wanna do for a living!"

"Wow, get a load of that Jenilee Jackalope," said Danny with a whistle. "Forget Demi Moone!"

Angela playfully slapped Danny's shoulder. "Oh, Danny, you're awful!"

***

Mark managed to change his major from theater to art, and when his family could no longer afford to keep him at Montevallo, he moved with them to a new house in Montgomery, where a community college actually offered a single course in Video Animation. That was something even his former college didn't have, so things seemed to be taking shape for the young animator.

Upon graduation, he got a job drawing cartoons for T-shirts. Although sports was something this young artist cared little for, at least drawing the mascots enabled him to move into his own apartment until he got a job as a multimedia specialist for training videos and making local animated commercials as a freelance animator. Thankfully, his animation professor from the local community college offered him a job teaching the Video Animation class as an adjunct instructor. It was just a couple of nights a week, but at least he was teaching animation to college students.

One afternoon after work, he spotted an article in *Animators Magazine*. William Richards, the animation director for *Who Drew Jeremy Jackalope?*, was offering an animation workshop in San Francisco. Much to his surprise, the training department at his job offered to send him on the trip, as he was animating the company mascot for a training video!

Upon meeting Richards, Mark informed him, "When

I saw Jeremy, I said to myself, 'Animation! That's what I wanna do for a living.'"

"Well, thank you," replied Richards, shaking Mark's hand firmly. He wore a bemused smile as he slicked back his graying temples with the other hand. "Thank you very much!"

Regrettably, the company Mark worked for later announced that, due to a change in their corporate leadership, they were moving their headquarters across the country to Oregon. Mark had little desire to leave his family, so he stayed behind, but soon found another job working computer graphics during the local newscast of the public television station. During this time, something extraordinary happened.

He met a girl named Lisa.

Tall, with soft brown eyes and wavy, reddish-brown hair, she was far more captivating than any other girl he had approached.

When they met at the singles group of his church, this beautiful girl, Lisa, told him she was from Costa Rica—and somehow, he knew *she* was the one. She was an artist!

After five years of attending the same young singles group, she was the first *artist* he had met, and before he knew it, they were dating. In just under a year, the young couple married in the same room in which they met.

Five years later, when she got a generous job offer in Atlanta, Mark told her to accept it, if that's what she really wanted, because of one single thought that immediately occurred to him: *Atlanta? That's where the Atlantamation Station is located!*

But if the young cartoonist thought getting a job there would be easy, he was wrong.

It would be a struggle, indeed.

Getting a job in Atlanta's TV stations proved to be much more competitive than it had been in Montgomery, so Mark had to accept an office job for a moving company just so they could afford to move into a comfortable two-bedroom unit with their two dogs, Guzy and Yoki. They later added two parakeets. It was plenty of room for a couple and their four small pets.

But it was soon to prove not enough for Mark's cartoon characters.

CHAPTER ONE:
Oh, Grow Up

Lisa set down Mark's screenplay as her husband studied her reaction carefully. She walked around his cluttered studio, the walls plastered with cartoon and movie posters, the shelves overflowing with drawing books and supplies. At least he was finally showing some progress toward cleaning up the long-standing mess.

"So, what do you think?" Mark asked. She had almost forgotten the question, so he was asking a second time.

"Not bad," she said. "It's just a little . . . more like a beginning. Nothing really happens that justifies a screenplay. A beginning without a middle and end. Good setup, but it doesn't . . ." She sighed and paused for dramatic effect. She looked away toward the clusters of action figures on the crowded bookshelves, trying her best not to get distracted by his messy studio, then back at her husband. She didn't want to hurt his feelings, but couldn't think of any other way to end her sentence. "It doesn't pay off."

"Like most of my cartoons, right?" Mark rubbed his forehead and sat back in the chair of his art desk, leaning back so far that Lisa wondered why he didn't fall over. *Sometimes it looks like he* can *defy gravity,* she thought.

"Like most of your cartoons," she said out loud.

Thinking she agreed with his last statement, Mark sighed. "I wish you weren't right."

"No honey, I didn't mean—"

"I just never know what to work on! I've tried comic strips, teen fantasy novels, short stories, some underground comic books. I even got that job as a colorist for that comic-book studio back in Montgomery!"

"I don't remember you ever mentioning that," Lisa replied. "Why didn't you ever tell me?"

"Because it only lasted about two weeks," Mark answered with yet another sigh.

"And you got let go?"

"Hmph, the company went under. I guess that's what comes of trying to start a comic-book studio in Montgomery."

"Just confirmed why we needed to move over here to Atlanta," Lisa said. "Better opportunities for both of us."

"Well, at least I've got my first animation class at the college here starting next week." Mark shrugged, a hopeful look on his face.

His wife shook her head. "Mark, might I remind you, you were already teaching one animation class a *year* before we moved from Montgomery. You had a solid job as creative services director at the TV station. Didn't you enjoy making those TV commercials?"

"Yeah, making those boring TV commercials— those boring, *disposable* live-action TV commercials. I was thirty-five and that's as far as I was gonna go in that town. When you got a job offer in Atlanta, my first thought was—"

They both looked up and exclaimed dreamily, "The Atlantamation Station!"

"And I'm so close. So close!" Mark leaned forward, propping his chin in his hand. "That college is right across the street from the Atlantamation Station! You think that's a coincidence?"

"I *know* it's a coincidence. That's what a coincidence *is*, sweetheart!" Lisa insisted. Mark rolled his eyes and she patted his arm soothingly. "Why don't you ask Lindsey for more classes in graphic design? That's more solid, anyway. You could even teach full time, with benefits."

"Graphic design?" Mark gave a guttural groan. "That's not why I moved here. I wanna draw cartoons, and I've at least won a Telly Award already for my animation."

"Right, I know, for your *Bigfoot Country* cartoon. I love your little blue cartoon skunk as much as anybody, but . . ."

Mark gave Lisa a disapproving stare. "The *porcupine* is blue, dear. Thurman. Thurman Q. Porcupine. You like Thurman. Deadbeat is the rascally skunk."

"Right. My point is, you can always keep working on these guys after supper while I call my mother back home. But during the day, you've gotta face it. You need a real job. I can help you with the cable bill, but that's it. We agreed before we moved here, the rent and the rest of the bills are your responsibility, dear. I have to pay for my mother's house in Montgomery. Unless, of course . . ."

Mark's eyes widened in mock terror. "Oh, no. Not even funny. Don't even say it."

"Unless of course . . . you'd like for me to sell the house in Montgomery, so she could move. . . back in with us?" Lisa fluttered her eyelashes sweetly.

Mark, temporarily defeated, snatched out a roll of packing tape and prepared to seal his box of sketchpads shut. "No, no. The first six years of our marriage was enough." He stopped and leaned on the box with a sarcastic grin. "Say, honey. What happened to that sweet, beautiful mural painter I fell in love with at the church singles group?"

Lisa returned a mirthless smile. "She had to grow up and get a real job as an architect. It's what we all have to do sometimes, dear. We all have to grow up."

"Well," Mark confessed, "at least you're good at both."

She offered him a more reassuring smile. "You coming to bed?"

"Yeah, just a minute." His eyes shot down to the box of memories. "I guess I really do need to get this box of old sketchbooks ready for storage."

"'Atta boy. See you in there." Lisa blew him a kiss on the way out, then left his studio.

Mark exhaled heavily and put his head on the desk. He looked over at the Telly Award, giving off a dim gleam among the action figures and art supplies crowding his shelf.

"Aw, what do those guys know? Anybody can win one of *those* things." Mark yanked it off the shelf, putting it into the box. Beside the empty award's resting spot was an autographed movie magazine, which he paused to inspect. He picked up the old issue of *Fearyville Monsters Magazine* with Forrest J. Ackerman, the publisher, on the cover, and prepared to put it in the box, as well.

Mark looked at the cover with a soft, nostalgic grin. "I still remember what you told me when I met you at the Atlanta Fantasy Fair . . . 'Mr. Ackerman, I always enjoyed reading your monster magazines before I grew up.' And what did you say?"

For a moment, it almost looked as if Forrest J. Ackerman's photo were talking to him, as he recalled the elderly gentlemen jokingly scolding, "Oh, no, no, *no*, young man. You should *never* grow up!"

Mark smiled broadly for a moment, then let it dissolve even more quickly. "Yeah, well, that's easy advice coming from a bachelor with a mansion packed full of movie-monster memorabilia. But for a married guy living in a two-bedroom apartment with barely enough room for a couple of small dogs and a pair of parakeets . . . maybe it *is* time to grow up."

He tossed the magazine into the box, facedown,

and took out the packing tape once again, but couldn't seem to bear closing it. He pulled out the sketchbook.

"Okay, one last glance, just for old time's sake. Then it's off to the storage closet, fellas."

Mark flipped through the sketchbook and glanced over his drawings. He paused at a portrait of a wild-haired creature with what looked like walrus tusks protruding from a duck-billed snout, and insane, concentric-circled eyes. A shaggy torso extended beneath a tight-fitting, striped undershirt to a pair of clawed, web feet. "Weird, I don't remember drawing that one in *color*," he said, noticing the red rims around the character's deranged eyeballs.

The pupils, focused forward, darted to look at their creator. The eyelids seemed to squint.

"Wait, did his eyes just . . . *move*? Nah."

Mark turned the page before his imagination got the best of him. It really *was* getting late.

"Well, even I gotta admit, not all my ideas were exactly 'comedy gold,'" he confessed. "Who would've thought a psychopathic platypus as a villain was funny?"

He flipped further through the sketchbook and stopped on a rough sketch of the *Bigfoot Country* comic strip.

"Wow, I thought I had it all figured out." He stared at the ceiling, grinning widely. "Start it with a comic strip, like good ol' Sparky Schulz, get it made into a holiday special, then start rollin' around in the royalty checks." He sighed deeply. "Just doesn't always work out like we plan though, does it, Deadbeat? Sorry, buddy. Sorry, Thurman, Sezquatch . . . and Girth Grizzly, ya big lug."

Mark lowered his head over the sketches and noticed a gap on Deadbeat. "Well, that'll never do. Missed a spot. Let me get that for you, pal." He reached over, plucked a pencil from his art caddy, then completed and darkened the single line. He shook his head and struggled to close the book. "I still can't do it."

He stood up and rubbed his forehead. "There was always something special about this sketchbook. I'm not sure why, but . . . maybe because every one of my favorite back-burner projects is sampled in there. But I'm afraid if I put you guys in storage, you're gonna be abandoned for good, just another batch of dead-end, back-burner projects like all those crazy fantasy-adventure novels I wrote as a teenager."

Mark clenched his fists so tight they hurt, fighting anger, fighting tears, fighting all the frustration an artist feels when he can't translate the ideas to paper and the means to making a living doing something he loved. It was exhausting.

He was finally ready to give up.

It felt like every ounce of creative energy he'd ever known was finally spent.

"I thought I had it all figured out for all of us. I really did. Sorry, fellas. I just hate for this to be . . . goodbye." Mark's eyes glistened in the light of his desk lamp. He leaned his head on top of the sketchbook, and a single tear rolled down his cheek to land on the *Bigfoot Country* drawing.

Mark wasn't sure if he had fallen asleep at first, but without a doubt, he felt the page beneath his face, then the sketchbook, and finally his whole art desk as they shook violently. The page began to flicker and flutter like a flag in the wind before a thunderstorm. His eyes widened and he looked down. The page slapped him in the face.

"Owww!" he exclaimed, suddenly angry. "What'd you do that fo—Hey, what . . .?"

Mark sat up as the page rippled and a single cartoon hand drawing stretched out of the paper. As it reached into the air, it solidified and turned jet black. A purple outline surrounded the hand as it stretched toward him.

Mark backed away against the wall, knocking over a shelf of action figures. He momentarily turned away from the drawing board to pick up the fallen toys.

"Here, I got it for ya, boss," offered a voice behind him.

It sounded so natural at first, the very voice he had recorded himself (not being able to afford professional voice actors) for the *Bigfoot Country* cartoon he had made nearly five years before. His involuntary reaction was to respond politely, almost without thinking, "Thanks, Deadbeat."

After all, he would know that skunk's voice anywhere.

Mark dropped the action figures, and his jaw followed.

He turned around slowly, knowing exactly who was standing there.

Deadbeat Skunk, the character from his cartoon strip, was standing in his studio, barely over three feet tall and grinning mischievously. He wiggled his eyebrows, unsettling the black, triangular pair of cowlicks above, one slightly bigger than the other. "Don't mention it, boss."

"Deadbeat, how did you get here?" exclaimed Mark.

A silly cartoon-music sting from seemingly nowhere jolted them both, and they looked around.

"And where did that crazy music come from?" asked Mark.

Deadbeat shrugged. "I don't know. It follows me wherever I go. You'll get used to it, and before you know it, you won't even notice it anymore. So, I wouldn't worry about it, boss. Besides, knowing you, it's probably royalty-free, anyway . . . right?"

Mark started to respond, but again his sketchbook rattled around from its wire-bound spine resting on the table. Out popped Thurman, the blue cartoon porcupine. Shaped like a gigantic robin's egg covered in quills, he rolled off the desk, landed on the floor with a thud, and shook himself. Cartoon stars swirled around his head as he stood up and slapped his whiskered snout, trying to uncross his eyes.

Deadbeat grunted in annoyance and crossed his arms. "Speaking of following me wherever I go . . ."

"Oh, that figures," Thurman sighed, shaking his head. "Wherever that crazy skunk goes, I have to follow and keep him out of trouble, I guess. Oh, I miss our forest already."

Mark pulled at his sideburns, unsettling and then adjusting his glasses. "Okay. Okay, my characters . . . got out of my sketchbook . . . somehow. Two dogs, two parakeets, two cartoons, in a two-bedroom apartment. Could be worse, I guess. They're forest animals, no more than . . . three feet tall, not so bad for cartoon characters. It could be worse, after all. Maybe if one of my bigger characters got out, like—"

"Like, oh, I dunno, maybe the namesake of our comic strip?" Deadbeat offered, with his trademark snarky grin. "A comic strip named . . .?"

With a resounding *THUMP*, all three turned toward the drawing desk. With three more thumps, they witnessed a giant orange bigfoot emerge.

"*Bigfoot Country*," Mark and his two new cartoon sidekicks said in chorus.

Mark, Deadbeat, and Thurman gazed up at the oversized ape in amazement.

"Ouch!" Sezquatch exclaimed, bumping his head against the ceiling. Squinting in temporary pain, he looked down at the others.

"Funny, most celebrities are usually shorter when you meet 'em in person," observed Deadbeat.

Looking down and around at his new indoor environment, Sezqautch muttered, "Hi, Professor. Um . . . I don't think we're supposed to be here."

"You guys know I'm a professor?" their creator asked.

"Sure, why not? You used to carry that sketchbook with you everywhere," answered Thurman with a happy shrug. "Prof. Mark, meet the star of your comic strip, A. Sezquatch."

"Hmph. *Co*-star, actually," Deadbeat corrected the porcupine, with a roll of his eyes.

"I wonder where Girth Grizzly is," said Thurman.

"So do I," agreed a confused voice behind them.

Deadbeat, Thurman, Sezquatch, and Prof. Mark turned around to see that Girth, a grizzly bear almost as large as Sezqatch, had appeared in the studio.

"I'm here, and don't even know where *here* is." The cartoon grizzly scratched his furry noggin.

Suddenly, the sketchbook started to quiver, and a succession of yet more characters began popping out.

"Oh, no, no, *no!*" exclaimed Prof. Mark. "How many more of you guys are gonna pop out here? I don't have room! This is just a two-bedroom apartment, for cryin' out loud! We're not even supposed to have the dogs here!"

"Is that . . . can it be . . . a *lady* porcupine?" whispered Thurman dreamily.

Sure enough, Petrol Jelly, another porcupine, had popped out and landed on the floor, pointing a laser blaster around suspiciously. Unlike the small, egg-shaped Thurman, however, Petrol was a tall, curvy, anthropomorphic female dressed as a futuristic rocket pilot. From behind her, a pair of mischievous-looking space squirrels peeked around her boots.

"Petrol Jelly and the Arsonist Space Squirrels?" Prof. Mark massaged his temples. "Oh, this won't end well."

"Nice to meet you, Prof. Mark," said Krispy, the green-furred squirrel with a toothy grin. He was easily distinguishable from his companion Krunchy, who wore an upside-down fishbowl on his head as a makeshift space helmet. "Say, uh, you don't happen to have a match, do you?"

"No, Prof. Mark. *No.*" Petrol Jelly shoved the squirrel aside. "The answer to this little fire hazard, and that question, is always *no.*"

Again, the sketchbook began to jiggle, and again, another character emerged, this one flailing her winged underarms around in a celebratory dance. Jayle, another anthropomorphic female, leaped out. Her large ears curved gracefully outward from her jet-black hair, tied into a ponytail with an oversized yellow bow. She danced about dressed in a sagging T-shirt. Bat wings emerged from her sleeves. She hopped out into their midst, dancing around in her denim cutoffs. She looked like she was just getting back from a college beach party. Prof. Mark even thought he noticed some cartoon sand flecking off her bare orange feet.

She didn't seem to notice the rest of them at first. "Whoo-hoo! Spring break 1992!" she exclaimed. "Daytona Beach, here I—Wait, where am I?" Her large, green eyes gazed helplessly around her.

"*When* are you?" huffed Petrol Jelly, crossing her gloved arms and studying the new arrival. "You're about thirteen years late for that particular spring break, sister. But judging from that oversized hairdo, I'd have guessed another *decade* or two . . ."

"Well, well, Prof. Mark," Deadbeat said. "Why don't you introduce me to *this* lovely creature? She must've been a couple pages back."

"This is Jayle," explained Prof. Mark. "She's obviously a bat. She's from a spring-break shirt back from when I was working for the T-shirt company. How can we stop you guys from popping out?"

"You're asking the wrong guy, boss. I just work here. So, Jayle, is it? Well, since it seems as if we'll be sharing an apartment, we might as well get to know one another . . ." Deadbeat grinned widely and Jayle shrank back, looking uncomfortable.

The sketchbook shook again, and out popped Marty the Gargoyle, a green-winged monster in a brown-fur loincloth with a skinny stegosaurus tail, wiggling his Groucho Marx–inspired eyebrows. "Hiya, Mark. Uh, kinda small quarters for a big imagination like yours, isn't it?"

"Easy, O Winged One," Deadbeat warned the

latest arrival. "There's only room enough for one wise-crackin' wise guy in this studio apartment, and that's me! Besides, I was here first, and I'm not goin' anywhere, *pal*!"

"Hey, he wrote the first draft of *my* novel when he was fourteen," the gargoyle bragged, "and sketched me before *that* when he was thirteen. Beat that, Stinky!"

"Oh-ho-ho, Stinky, is it?" Deadbeat closed his eyes and rubbed his temples, his tail starting to quiver. "If you want Stinky, pal, believe me, I can help you out there!"

"Oh, no, you don't!" exclaimed Sezquatch as Thurman and Girth grabbed Deadbeat and wrapped the skunk's tail around him in a makeshift straitjacket. "Not again."

"I'm not taking another round of tomato-juice baths for three weeks," grumbled Thurman. "Not after last time."

"I'm not one to question our creator," said Sezquatch to Prof. Mark, "but would it have been too much trouble to draw him as a badger?"

"Or a caribou!" suggested Thurman.

"Or a bunny rabbit!" giggled Girth Grizzly. "A cute little, fluffy bunny rabbit."

All the characters began arguing, and Prof. Mark looked around wildly. "Oh, boy, the only way this could get any worse is if my wife would hear all this commo—"

Prof. Mark stopped midsentence and looked down at Thurman, who was staring at him more like a cartoon deer in the headlights than a porcupine. Thurman gulped, and pointed behind the cartoonist.

"My wife's standing *right* behind me, isn't she, Thurman?" asked Prof. Mark.

"Yup," replied Thurman, still not blinking.

"My day is officially complete," Prof. Mark muttered.

It looked as though Lisa had managed to fall asleep just prior to the disturbance in Mark's studio, as she was rubbing her eyes, obviously groggy. "Mark, would you please turn down that iMac of yours? The speakers *are* impressive, but I thought you said you were coming to . . . bed . . ."

She paused, looking around at the strange assortment of cartoon characters. Thurman blushed purple, and waved at her bashfully.

"Oh, hey, honey," offered Prof. Mark. "I was just about to put that box of sketchbooks away in storage, just like you asked, as you probably recall, when the *funniest* darn thing happened. . . "

Her eyes widened farther than he thought humanly possible with every passing syllable of his explanation. He looked around helplessly, having forgotten whatever else he was about to say. Under the circumstances, he decided introductions were in order. "Lisa, meet my cartoon characters. My cartoon characters, my wife, Lisa. Um, say hi, everybody. . ."

"Hi, everybody!" replied his characters in an almost deafening chorus.

Before Lisa could manage a reaction, Deadbeat zipped to a stop in front of her with an obligatory puff of cartoon smoke. "Wow, boss, you really did well for yourself," he mumbled sideways, before grabbing her hand in preparation for a kiss. "Hello, gorgeous. I'm Deadbeat Skunk, and I don't believe we've been formally introduced, m'lady, but—"

Lisa yanked her hand backward and stumbled away from Deadbeat before he could finish. She took another look at all the grinning, wild-eyed characters and gasped, bordering on hyperventilating. "Hello, all of you, and welcome to the . . . *third* dimension, and if you'll excuse me, I have to do something very important . . . I just have to . . . faint . . ."

Her eyes rolled back in her head and she promptly fainted. Girth, who happened to be standing nearest, managed to catch her limp form. "Hey, Prof. Mark, I think your wife fainted . . . just like she said she would." He looked down at her with an impressed grin. "Hm. Good call."

"Yeah, well . . . thanks, Girth." Prof. Mark began to fan her with a comic book.

No one seemed to notice that once again, the sketchbook on the table was trembling. But this time, something was different. The desk lamp flickered and dimmed, then seemed to pulse with a dark-green life of its own.

"Is she okay?" exclaimed Jayle, kneeling down by Lisa's side.

"Stand back and give her some air, civilians!" ordered Petrol Jelly. "Secure the perimeter!"

"You want me to give her mouth-to-mouth?" offered Deadbeat.

"Deadbeat!" Jayle and Petrol shouted simultaneously.

The space ranger cocked her laser pistol. Deadbeat backed away respectfully.

A gnarled green hand emerged from the sketchbook as the desk lamp went out entirely. A wild-haired shadow began to emerge as the matching hand grasped the other side of the table and began to pull itself into the art studio.

A webbed foot flopped down onto the plastic carpet guard beside the desk, and a single spur—something like a rooster's, but more like that of a velociraptor—flicked out in a single motion and glimmered menacingly in the dim light from the hallway.

Thurman happened to glance over toward the sound. "I'd know that sound anywhere—it's a poison *platypus* spur!" he whispered with a gulp. His eyes widened and locked onto the hypnotic gaze of the wicked, concentric-circled eyes glaring at him from the shadows. "Uh, guys," he said, his voice rasping. "Guys, oh fellas . . . Deadbeat? Sezquatch? P-puh . . . Prof. Mark?" he sputtered.

"Thurman, what?" shouted Deadbeat. "Can't you see we've got problems here?"

"Guys, we've got bigger problems—*there!*" whimpered Thurman, turning Deadbeat's head to face the new arrival.

Although cloaked in shadow, the dark figure's eyes seemed to be illuminated from an eerie fire within. Beneath was a jagged grin, the two most prominent teeth much like those of a saber-toothed tiger jutting out in front of all the others.

"Um, could be worse," Deadbeat offered half-heartedly.

"How could it possibly be worse than an axe-wielding, psychopathic platypus cartoon loose in my art studio, Deadbeat?" exclaimed Prof. Mark.

"Well," the skunk continued, "at least he's the only villain to escape your sketchb-b-boo—"

All the characters gasped in unison as they gazed behind the menacing platypus.

He had not arrived alone.

And unlike the other characters that had emerged from the sketchbook, whatever this dark creature was, it continued to grow until the furry tufts of its long ears reached the ceiling . . .

And still continued to grow.

Then, just when they thought the creature could grow no further, the ceiling buckled and gave way to the enormous, unforgivable mass of the roaring, raging beast beneath.

And then the ceiling disappeared.

CHAPTER TWO:
Roommates by the Dozen

Mercifully, Lisa had fainted and missed all the mayhem that followed. All she ever knew was that, moments later, Prof. Mark and Sezquatch had moved her to the couch in their living room and put a cold rag on her forehead.

"Oh, Mark, I had the strangest dream," she said as she awoke. "I dreamed I walked into your studio and saw all your . . ."

"All my cartoon characters walking around, I know." Prof. Mark scratched his head.

"What? How did you know what I was dream—" Lisa began.

"It wasn't exactly a dream, gorgeous," interrupted Deadbeat. "We're all still here, nice and cozy."

Lisa looked around, just as confused as before.

"I believe you know my *Bigfoot Country* characters," Prof. Mark said. "Deadbeat, Sezquatch, Girth Grizzly, and of course, Thurman."

"Thurman? Yes, he's my favorite. Oh, he's so sweet, really, but . . ."

Deadbeat crossed his arms. "Blatant favoritism," he muttered with a disgusted snort.

"Petrol and the Arsonist Space Squirrels, you may not know them," Prof. Mark continued. "Jayle, of course, from that beach-party T-shirt. You don't know

Marty the Gargoyle. He was from a series of fantasy novels I wrote as a teenager. Dr. Ratnest arrived while you were out—"

"Dr. Victor Vincent Van Von Ratnest, at your service, my dear," said a tall blue rat in a yellow lab uniform, kissing her hand. "And I am simply *charmed* to make the acquaintance of such a ravishing young woman. I believe it was the bard Sir William Shakespeare himself who told us—"

"Excuse me, Dr. Ratnest," Lisa stopped him. "How exactly . . . did all this happen?"

"I'm not exactly sure *how* it happened," Prof. Mark said. "But I think it had something to do with that last sketchbook I was about to put away. Thankfully only a dozen got out before we closed the box."

"*Only* a dozen?" exclaimed Lisa. "Mark, honey, we aren't even supposed to have the *dogs* here, much less a dozen . . . wait a minute." Lisa began to look around her and count. "The *Bigfoot Country* characters, that's four. The other porcupine, the two squirrels, and the bat, that's eight. The gargoyle and the lab rat makes ten . . . where are the *other* two?"

Prof. Mark looked at Sezquatch nervously.

"Mrs. Toonery, why don't you try one of these chocolate éclairs I made while you were out?" the bigfoot suggested. "Sometimes tough news is easier to take on a full stomach."

"Tough news?" said Lisa. "We were comfortably settled in this apartment in a new city, at our new jobs, and now we have to share our apartment with your *cartoon* characters. And there's *more* tough news?" She grabbed Deadbeat, who was nearest, and began shaking him feverishly.

"Is all this cartoon violence necessary for a simple question?" he said.

Lisa continued, eyeing the skunk fiercely, "Where are the other two? Are they bigger than Sezquatch?"

Suddenly the entire apartment shook with a rolling shockwave. "Well, *one* of them is," confessed Deadbeat with a smug grin.

Another *thud* followed, and another. Books fell off the shelves. The dogs started barking, and the parakeets twittered nervously.

"Please don't tell me those were *footsteps*," Lisa said to Deadbeat.

Deadbeat shrugged, and with a single motion swiped a cartoon zipper across his mouth. For once, he kept his mouth shut.

After two more thuds, Lisa turned to Thurman. "They *are* footsteps, Mrs. Toonery," he confessed. "Woe unto us all."

Lisa turned back to Deadbeat, who unzipped his mouth. "Well, you told *me* not to tell you," he muttered.

Everyone turned to the hallway, where a gigantic foot landed on the carpet. It looked something like an eagle's claw, but covered with shaggy brown hair . . . and it was about forty feet long. For the moment, the thought scarcely had time to enter Lisa's mind that the apartment hallway had originally been less than *half* that length. She barely noticed that the hallway, and the very walls, seemed to buckle like an outlandish, warped camera effect to make way for the gigantic, monstrous foot. It rose up out of view and continued down the hallway to the bathroom, where the door closed. The pets calmed down once the footsteps had faded.

"What," gasped Lisa, clutching a sofa cushion for protection, "was *that*?"

"*That* was Zhae-Garr," explained the gargoyle. "He came from the same series of fantasy stories I was in, but he predates me by several thousand years. I gotta hand it to your husband, Mrs. T., he sure knows how to make a back-story for his characters."

"I don't care about back-stories, or exposition, or—" Lisa began.

"Well, it could be worse," offered Deadbeat. "It's not like he brought over a carnivorous dinosaur from *Jurassic Carnivore Carnival*, right?"

"Oh," sighed Lisa, almost with relief, "so that thing doesn't eat meat?"

"Well, actually, he does," began Prof. Mark, scratching the back of his neck. "Well, he is carnivorous, yes."

"Well, he's not as big as one of those dinosaurs, right?" asked Deadbeat.

"Um, he is actually bigger than *most* dinosaurs, yeah," explained Prof. Mark. "By about, uh . . ."

"Nearly five hundred feet taller, by most accounts of the fossil record," noted Dr. Ratnest. "However, if you'd rather—"

"What?" snapped Lisa. "If I'd rather *what*?" Her

nostrils flared, and she leaned threateningly toward the scientist, almost another foot taller than her.

Dr. Ratnest cleared his throat awkwardly. "No, I don't suppose you would be interested in me translating that into *meters*, would you?"

Lisa scoffed and turned away, rolling her eyes.

"Well, on the bright side, he—" began Prof. Mark. Lisa's glare shot in his direction. "Never mind."

"Is there a *bright* side, dear?" Lisa inquired.

"Well, he is actually intelligent," Prof. Mark offered. "He speaks several languages, including what we call English, and—"

"So," Lisa replied with a sigh that finally resembled relief, "he can be reasoned with?"

Prof. Mark rubbed the side of his chin. "Well, of sorts, now that you mention it. Okay, well, not *quite* so much, no . . . he is under the impression that he's some sort of ancient god, or some such."

"Well, I guess if you draw a malevolent, carnivorous supervillain taller than certain metropolitan skyscrapers, then he's *bound* to have some sorts of delusions of grandeur, wouldn't you say? Of course!" Lisa thrust her hands onto her hips, practically daring anyone else to elaborate.

"Well, it would stand to reason," Dr. Ratnest agreed cautiously, "that if Zhae-Garr had—"

"Jay . . ." Lisa interrupted, her lower lip quivering, "Garr?"

"No, honey, it *rhymes* with Jay," Prof. Mark interrupted helpfully, "but it's got a sort of softer beginning, like a cross between a *j* and a *sh* sound."

"I don't care *how* you pronounce it," Lisa said, standing up. "I want *it*, and all the other ten of your little outlined—"

"Eleven," corrected Deadbeat.

"Deadbeat!" everyone shouted.

The skunk shrugged. "Hey, don't blame me! I didn't draw it! *Somebody's* gonna have to tell her what's in the linen closet sooner or later."

Everyone in the room looked more uncomfortable than they had yet.

"Well, honey, it's—" Prof. Mark began.

"No, Mr. Toonery," Dr. Ratnest interrupted. "This new denizen of your domicile is not *your* responsibility, but mine, and my shame alone, so I had best explain."

"Wait a minute. I *do* recognize you," said Lisa. "You're that evil scientist from . . ."

Dr. Ratnest scowled, his fur bristling. "Not *evil* scientist, necessarily. I prefer the term *mad* scientist, if we must dwell in the character clichés we are assigned."

"Then whatever's in that closet is worse than a five-hundred-foot-tall whatsit in my bathroom? What could *possibly* be worse?"

Something like a raging cougar snarl, followed by an icy chuckle, echoed down the hallway. All the characters froze, petrified.

"What," Lisa finally said, breaking the silence, "w-what is in my linen closet?" She peered around the corner, where a pair of luminous eyes peeped between two broken slats in the closet door.

"Hello, hello," sang a dazed voice that sounded

more like a wacky, mostly harmless cartoon character. "If you're so terri-bibbly curious as to what's in your closet, maybe what's in your closet is quite feral-ociously curious in having a closer look at *you*, hm? Why don't you come a little closer, and let me have a look at you?"

Lisa leaned farther around the corner. As she did so, there was an outburst of snarls and roars, followed by another round of icy chuckles, which died off into silence.

"Tell me that's not . . ." Her lip trembled even more than before.

"Daggur Bill Platypus," sighed Dr. Ratnest, wagging his head. "Once the most dedicated investigation agent for the IRS in our cartoon world, until he came to audit me at my hilltop castle, and . . . well, he became the first experiment in my Electro-Genetricide Chair. You see, it augments any cosmetic surgery its occupant has undergone, and Bill had dental implants, which turned into—"

A pair of large tusks, something like those of a walrus, shot out from the hole in the closet door and gnawed feverishly on the edges of the slats.

"He can't get out of there, can he?" said Lisa. "I know cartoon characters can do just about anything—"

"Strange thing I've noted about your universe," said Dr. Ratnest. "We've maintained many of our cartoon abilities from our own world—or worlds, if you like—but thankfully, some of the basic laws of *your* world, the inevitability of gravity and such, still hold dominion over us—if only with a slight delay. I've made some further modifications to the structure besides, as best I could without my lab equipment. Daggur Bill would have to be *let* out somehow . . . but no one here would be *foolish* enough to do such a thing, as we all know how dangerous he is."

"I don't care about *keeping* him there. I want him *back* on the drawing board," Lisa said. "Why don't you just get rid of him altogether? Can't you just get a gigantic eraser, or something?"

Dr. Ratnest restrained himself from giving Lisa a disdainful glare, but just barely. "Dear lady, this isn't a Jeremy Jackalope cartoon, you know."

"Honey, I don't know if I could get rid of *any* of them, even if I wanted to," Prof. Mark confessed. "I don't even know how they got here, much less how to put them *back*."

"We should just make the best of our astonishing situation, Mrs. Toonery," Dr. Ratnest explained. "It would seem that once you create an idea, it's difficult, if not downright impossible, to destroy it—even a bad idea. That's why we have to be careful about the ideas we come up with and letting them out where people can see them."

"The first thing we better decide," Prof. Mark suggested, "is how we'll manage the sleeping arrangements tonight."

"I've got dibs on the sleeper sofa," snapped Deadbeat quickly.

"I'll flip you for it," said Marty the Gargoyle. Grabbing Deadbeat by the tail, he added, "Heads I win, tails you lose!"

"Are you prayin' for a sprayin'?" said Deadbeat.

"Deadbeat, don't you dare spray anybody," Sezquatch warned. "I don't wanna start waving your blackmail material around these nice new folks."

And then everyone started yelling, squawking, and barking at the same time.

"Whoever thought being a cartoonist would be so darn *noisy*?" Prof. Mark shook his head sadly.

It was going to be a long night with their assortment of new roommates.

CHAPTER THREE:
What Lurked in the Linen Closet . . .
Has Escaped!

The next morning, Prof. Mark had an early class and Lisa had to go to work. Petrol was experienced in keeping the mischievous space squirrels in check, and Sezquatch likewise kept an eye on Deadbeat and Marty. The other characters were reasonably well-behaved, so it came down to Dr. Ratnest to keep an eye on the monster in the closet—Daggur Bill Platypus.

Dr. Ratnest approached the closet with Daggur Bill's breakfast, a hamburger.

"Oh, Bill," called Dr. Ratnest, politely rapping on the edge of the barricaded linen closet with his black-gloved knuckles. "Chow time, Daggur Bill."

The platypus snarled as his hand shot out between two broken slats of wood and snatched the hamburger. "Hey, c'mon, Doc," snapped Daggur Bill after a couple of quick slurps and one gulp. "Enough horsin' around. When ya gonna let me out of this lousy linen closet?"

"Sorry, Bill, but I gave our cartoonist my solemn word of honor," replied Dr. Ratnest. "And Dr. Vincent Van Von Ratnest may be a conniving, twisted, back-stabbing, underhanded, vile, contemptible turncoat . . . but . . . Ohhh . . . where *was* I going with that?" Dr. Ratnest paused, his back to the closet, scratching his head.

"Yeah, yeah, yeah," grumbled Bill. "Word of honor,

right. Now just cut the gravy already and let me outta here."

Dr. Ratnest waved his hands at his earlier ramblings. "Oh, never mind. Sorry, Bill. The point is, I gave my word to our cartoonist, and that's the end of the matter. You're not getting out. No one's letting you out. Neither I nor anyone here would be *foolish* enough to do such a thing. My apologies." He gave a final sniff, cleared his throat, and walked away.

Bill gave the nailed boards a series of frustrated rattles, snarling angrily. "Bah! Blast that blasted turncoat Ratnest," he muttered. "He and those other goody-goody cartoons can run free in that starving artist's apartment, while I'm cooped up in this stinkin' linen closet with barely three meals a day to sustain my raging appetite." Bill drummed his fingers and pulled his wild hair.

"What have I done to deserve this malici-ousness treatment? I didn't ask to look like this! That's it! It's all because of my appearance . . . Is it because I'm a saber-toothed platypus?"

"Gee, I dunno, Bill," said a feminine voice just outside the closet. "Maybe it's because you're an axe-wielding psychopath."

Bill peeked out between the wooden slats and saw Jayle Bat passing by. "Hey! Even us axe-wielding psy-chopaths have *feelings*, all right?" He crossed his arms, his wild eyes darting back and forth. "So even that Jayle Bimbo Bat wouldn't be dumb enough to let me out of this closet," he grumbled. "Neither would those dopey do-gooders from *Bigfoot Country* comics. Those space squirrels have some potential, but that pretty 'n pesky porcupine lady keeps them in check. The giant and Marty the Gargoyle barely make more than a campy cameo appearance anyhow. If only one of them were dumb enough to—"

"Do I hear a talking linen closet?" asked Girth Grizzly, eyeing the door warily.

"And then, without warning," mumbled Bill, just under his breath, "there was a light at the end of the tunnel. However *dim* . . ."

"Duhh, so who's in there, a talking washcloth?" asked Girth.

"No, it's me, the buxom damsel in distress," replied Bill, hastily disguising his voice as best he could. "Miss Jayle the Bat! Oh, boo-hoo!"

"Oh, hi, Miss Jayle," said Girth. "Gosh, you're so purty and sweet. But your voice is, uh . . ."

"Oh, ahem. Yes, I've been locked in this linen closet—accidentally, of course—and I've been screaming for help until my voice has become hoarse. I don't sound like myself at all."

"Say, you'd better be careful," Girth warned. "Prof. Mark keeps a big, dangerous duck-thing in one of these closets."

"That's *platypus*, you clod—" snarled Bill, but he caught himself. "Um, er, yes. Why don't you let some light in here and help me look inside? Maybe it's this very one . . ."

"Yeah, you may be right." Girth pulled the door

open, the nailed boards coming loose seemingly with-out effort. "But I better look quick, to see if he's hiding behind you."

As the hinges creaked and a board snapped free, Bill extended the tip of his webbed foot forward, grabbing a pair of towels to conceal himself, just in case. "Hmm, Christmas came early this year, folks," he chuckled lowly. "Oh, um, don't look, Girth! When I got trapped in the closet, I wasn't decent! Tee-hee!"

"Oh, gosh!" Girth exclaimed, blushing under his fur. "I don't wanna see *nobody* in a state of in-un-decency! So, don't worry. I'll cover my eyes until you're out."

"You've been such wonderful assistance to me, Girth. I've never met such a gentlemanly grizzly!"

Girth chuckled, his paws still over his eyes. "Aw, shucks."

Daggur Bill glared at the grizzly, then smiled as another idea dawned in his dark mind. While Girth's eyes were still covered, Daggur Bill crept past Prof. Mark's studio, where he spied the open sketchbook—the one from which they had all escaped—still on the artist desk, wound tightly with artist's tape.

Bill paused, listening.

A tremor shook the apartment. Zhae-Garr, the giant, was about to make another appearance in the hall-way. A wicked grin trickled across Daggur Bill's over-sized beak.

The platypus took the sketchbook, unwrapped the tape binding, and placed it open in the hallway, direct-ly in the path he knew Zhae-Garr would take. He tip-toed around behind Girth, still hiding his eyes as the giant's footsteps started getting louder.

"Uh-oh, it sounds like that giant monster is on the way again. Can I uncover my eyes yet, Miss Jayle?" asked Girth.

"No, not yet," said Bill, still doing an impersonation of the pretty bat. "But just so you know, I'm so scared, I'm covering my eyes, too!"

"Should I, uh, heh-heh, hold your hand to help you not be scared?" offered Girth shyly.

"Oh, no—let me hold *yours*," said Bill, pulling him back only slightly as the giant—or rather, his immense foot—made its appearance, heading straight for the open sketchbook.

Zhae-Garr's foot rose high in the air, far above the sketchbook, and for a moment, Daggur Bill doubted whether it would make his intended target. After a pair of seconds that seemed like a century to the wicked platypus, the foot plummeted downward and landed squarely on the open page.

For a split millisecond, it seemed the foot would continue on its journey down the hall, but just before that moment could begin, Zhae-Garr's weight became too much for the thin support of the sketchbook page. A dent, and then a tear, appeared beneath the clawlike foot, and the roaring giant sank straight downward, his furry arms waving angrily as he disappeared into the shuddering page.

Just before he sank down, he spun around and glared at Daggur Bill, one hand clutching at the edge of the torn page. The giant's face looked something like that of a monstrous, maned lynx, but with a boar's tusks and an ape's flattened nose. "You *platypus*," snarled the giant. Then he slid the rest of the way down, gone with a flash of light.

The sketchbook lay open, but now, on the open page, was a surprisingly small tear, less than an inch across in the upper corner—all that remained of the giant's passage.

"Is the giant gone now?" asked Girth once the roars of fury had stopped.

"Yep, the big goof is gone now," said Bill. "Now for the *other* one . . ."

"What was that last part?" Girth responded uncertainly.

"Okay, get ready to open your eyes, but stand right

here," said Daggur Bill. "And lean forward, just ever so slightly, if you please."

"Whatever you say, Miss Jayle," Girth chuckled. "I'd do near about just anything for a purty girl like you."

"Would you sail to the ends of the earth for me?" asked the platypus.

"You bet," said Girth.

"Funny you should say that," replied Daggur Bill, his voice returning to normal with growing menace, "because that's *exactly* what I had in mind."

"Hey, you don't sound like Miss Jayle anymore," said Girth. "In fact, I think you're *not* Miss Jayle at all!"

Daggur Bill wound his foot up to give Girth a kick just as the bear took his hands away from his eyes, but he was looking in the wrong direction.

Daggur Bill was behind him.

"Congratulations, furball! You win a prize!" cackled Bill.

"What prize is that?" asked Girth.

"An all-expenses-paid trip," growled the platypus, "back *home!*" Bill finished his web-footed windup and kicked Girth forward. His aim was flawless, and the grizzly went sailing forward, landing squarely on the ragged tear in the open sketchbook. Sadly, Girth went through even faster than the giant had, and disappeared almost instantly.

With another grim chuckle, the dangerous duckbill marched toward the living room, flexing his crooked fingers.

"Now, where did that pair of live-action losers hide my axe?"

He had a busy evening ahead of him.

CHAPTER FOUR:
Expert Advice

His afternoon class done, Prof. Mark looked both ways along the busy streets of Midtown Atlanta before crossing over. Watching the cars dash down the parallel streets, he could only imagine how long rush-hour traffic would take to get home after this meeting. A lonesome siren blared in the distance as he hurried to beat the crossing signal and huffed to a stop. He gazed up at the neon sign over the building that lay less than fifty feet across the intersection from Westwood College, where he taught four days a week. "Atlantamation Station," he read aloud. "Haven't been here since they rejected my *last* round of show pitches."

Almost in reply to his own comment, the darkening storm clouds above rumbled. The coming storm wouldn't make his trip home any easier.

Prof. Mark wearily released a long, drawn-out sigh as he approached the front door. He had remained on good terms with several of the staff there. Although he felt any chance of getting one of his own shows produced here was long gone, it seemed there was always hope his students might get jobs at their studio.

As he adjusted his collar, he regretted not wearing at least a light jacket, as the cool, late-afternoon breeze reminded him that fall was almost upon him. He tapped on the glass door and the security guard squinted, nodded as he recognized their infrequent visitor, and his hand disappeared beneath the desk to press the unseen button. At the signal of the buzzer, Prof. Mark pushed the door open and walked in.

"Well, Prof. Mark, it's been a while!" exclaimed the aging guard. "To what, may I ask, do we owe this unexpected pleasure?"

"Hiya, Jackson," Prof. Mark replied with a firm, sincere handshake. "You're right, it's been too long."

"I was afraid you'd given up. I really hoped one of these days the folks here would wise up and give one of your shows the greenlight! Especially that one with the . . . what was it, the bigfoot, that porcupine, and that rascally blue skunk! Aw, man, he was a character, all right!"

"He still is," agreed Prof. Mark. "Oh, and the, uh, porcupine's the blue one."

"What was his name? Thurman, right! Deadbeat's the skunk. Right you are, Professor," the guard added with a chuckle. "Can't wait to see those characters of yours running around over here, painted on the wall beside our others!" Jackson gestured grandly at the massive mural of cartoon characters lining the entrance.

"Well, that might happen sooner than you think," Prof. Mark confessed, grinning weakly.

"That's the spirit! Let's see now, who do we have you down to see?" Jackson ran his finger along a list of names on the clipboard.

"Dave Friendly," Prof. Mark said, hoping to get inside, remembering his wife alone with their numerous outlined roommates, if he didn't hurry home. "He's one of your new animation directors."

"Dave's a good guy. Yeah, where did you meet Dave?"

"The figure-drawing class on Thursday nights at Westwood," Prof. Mark said with a nod. "Across the street, actually."

"Oh, yeah, I see a lot of our animators head straight over there on Thursday nights," Jackson recalled. "Oh, and you do know Ms. Linda left us not long ago, right?"

"Well, she was the one who told us if anybody ever had an idea for a show, to schedule a visit," Prof. Mark said. "Her door was always open."

"Well, I hate to tell you, but to be honest,"—Jackson

looked from side to side and lowered his voice, as if the security cameras or painted characters could somehow overhear them—"the new executives here, they're not as open to *outside* ideas as Ms. Linda used to be."

"Well, Jackson, to be honest," Prof. Mark said, also lowering his voice, "I'm here about something more important than just to pitch another show idea."

Jackson grinned, impressed. "Well then, Prof. Mark, don't let me hold you back any longer. Right through those doors to the elevator, top floor, and Dave's office is two doors down the hall from where Ms. Linda's used to be."

"Thanks, Jackson." Prof. Mark picked up his pace and headed through the doors and to the elevator. "I better make this fast," he muttered to himself. "I don't think Lisa can handle being alone with those drawings of mine much longer."

***

Prof. Mark sat down across the desk from Dave Friendly, a pleasantly smiling artist with a thin beard and graying temples. "Sure glad you took the time to see me, Dave," Prof. Mark said as he admired the framed cartoon cels, animation posters, and action-figure collection lining the director's shelves and drawing desk. It was a collection that rivaled his own.

"Sure, we certainly appreciate you guys at the college making your figure-drawing room available to us on Thursdays," Dave said. "It's nice to walk across the street and draw for a couple of hours after work, without the deadlines—just draw for the fun of it!"

"Well, we do forget sometimes we became cartoonists for the sheer *fun* aspect," Prof. Mark agreed with a weary laugh.

Dave chuckled. "Yeah, the deadlines have a way of taking over, don't they? So, what can I do for you? You said it was something *like* a show idea, but not exactly . . . I was a little puzzled by your call."

"Well, say, for instance, there was a, uh, a show, right? About a guy whose cartoon characters start popping out of his sketchbook, and he has to share his two-bedroom apartment with all these characters and his wife." Prof. Mark paused, not knowing quite how to continue.

"Hm, now *that* might be an interesting pitch," Dave agreed. "You've got the cartoon and live-action angle like *Jeremy Jackalope*, but all the domestic conflict of the couple. So, kind of like *I Dream of Jenny*, but where they're hiding the cartoon characters from the landlord who doesn't like pets in sort of a farcical . . . hmm. And all the major action takes place in their apartment, you say? So essentially, we'd just have to build one live-action set, and two actors. And you do your own character voices, too, I recall. Not much of a budget problem, there. Execs would like that aspect, I can tell you that already. *Anything* to save a buck, these new suits—"

"But," Prof. Mark interrupted, "let's say it also involves the cartoonist. He's starting to, I dunno, maybe doubt his own *sanity*. Like maybe the characters *aren't* real—except, of course, his wife can see them and interact with them, too?"

"Yeah . . . this may be one of your strongest pitches yet." Dave smiled. "I am liking this, buddy! You may be on to something this time."

"You don't think the main character—the cartoonist, that is—could actually be *going* crazy, do you?" said Prof. Mark, rubbing the back of his neck.

"Well, no, not if the wife can see them, too," said Dave. "It does remind me of something, though . . . something that really happened on the set of *Jeremy Jackalope*."

"*You* worked on *Jeremy Jackalope*?" Prof. Mark gasped.

"Well, technically, I worked on his wife. Designing her character, I mean," Dave said. "But yeah, I did go to the set one day, and Rob Fleischer, the guy playing the detective, he was having a rough day."

"What happened?"

"Well, he and the stand-in for Jeremy, the guy reading the Jackalope's lines, were both method actors. Gary Lantz, the Jackalope actor, would stand there in this big furry suit, antlers and everything, to set up the shot, and then the camera would roll and he'd step out. And y'know, they'd superimpose the animated characters later in post-production. But Rob Fleischer would stand there and talk to these characters, even *after* each shot was over, making small talk with them like they were really there. You really *believed* him. But after the shoot was over, they said Fleischer had a near breakdown."

"What do you mean?"

"He had done this method-acting thing so long,

he was actually *seeing* these jackalopes and gangster ferrets after him. You know, some serious hallucinations. He later said to me, 'You spend six months dreaming up jackalopes and ferrets, they start to take over, you know?'"

"Wow . . . so it's not unheard of."

"And one day, the weirdest thing happened." Dave's eyes lit up suddenly.

"Yeah?" Prof. Mark leaned forward.

"Well, after one of the shots was over, I could have almost sworn, just for a couple of seconds, I *saw* that Jackalope standing there myself, nodding to Rob as he talked to him, just like in the movie. Complete with shadows and highlights, as solid as you are, sitting in that chair listening to me now. I turned to somebody beside me, asking me if they were using some kind of, I dunno, high-tech projector or something. But when I blinked and looked back, he was gone. Always figured I must have imagined it." Dave got a puzzled look on his face, as if remembering more. He shook his head and blinked again, as though he were trying to reforget the unsettling incident.

"Method actors, right?" said Dave with a chuckle, but he paused, getting a far-off look in his eye. "But one of our Asian animators said something, well, rather interesting . . ."

"Asian animators?"

"Well, he was Japanese. Half Japanese—his mother was from Tibet, I think. In Tibetan tradition, they have something called a *tulpa*."

"What's a *tulpa?*"

"Well, the Tibetan monks believe that with months of concentration and meditation, they can conjure up one of these *tulpas.* Sort of a mental image that becomes so real, so seemingly solid, that *other* people can see it."

"So, these *tulpas* . . . could they become so real they could actually talk, interact with others besides their creator, even pick up physical objects?"

"Well, after he got me interested, I did some reading," Dave continued. "A British folklore specialist or something, back in the 1920s, this lady scientist, found out about the *tulpas* while studying among the monks. She tried an experiment where, just to be safe, she would come up with this friendly, chubby little monk. And like Fleischer, after months of concentration, she could *see* him. Even was having a conversation with him in a tent during a pilgrimage, and another monk who stepped in apologized for interrupting her conversation with her . . . *friend.*"

"So, others *can* see them," Prof. Mark gasped.

"In certain cases, yes," Dave agreed. "But it didn't end well."

"What happened?"

"The folklorist said that over time, this happy little monk character developed sort of a twisted grin and a mischievous sense of humor to go along with it. Over time, she felt she had unleashed something downright malevolent."

"Oh, no. *Bill,*" said Prof. Mark.

"What's that? Who's Bill?" asked Dave.

"Daggur Bill, he's a saber-toothed platypus," Prof. Mark explained. "He's the villain—well, in the *story*."

"Oh, yeah," Dave agreed. "I like that. That's a good element of conflict, just the spice your story needs. A snaggletooth platypus."

"Saber-toothed," Prof. Mark corrected. "But snaggle-tooth? Yeah, he's got a few of those, too, I guess."

"That could be what you've been missing. Adds a real sense of *menace* to the story."

"You don't know *how* real," Prof. Mark replied.

"Yeah, a duckbill platypus with fangs," Dave said. "That just might appeal to the tween crowd—our target demographic. You just might be on to something with this story, Prof. Mark!"

Prof. Mark started getting up. "I might have gone too far with it already, I'm afraid. I better be going before *it* goes any further."

"Oh, no, you're definitely on the right track with this one," said Dave. "If you need to beat this traffic, that's fine, as I'm about to head home myself. But we are *not* done talking about this idea of yours, Professor. I really want to help you get this one on the air. You've been a struggling cartoonist long enough."

"Thanks, Dave. You've been more help than you know!" Prof. Mark said, heading out the door.

"Oh, one more thing before you go," Dave said, getting up and following. "There's something I could use *your* help with."

"What's that?" Prof. Mark's eyes darted toward the door.

"You know anything about this new animation program called Flash?"

"Yeah, I've got a beta version. I've played around with it a little."

"I've got a publisher friend in Texas, and he's looking for someone to write a user's manual on it. I figure with your writing experience and your teaching qualifications, you would be just the guy for the job."

"Yeah, that sounds great! Can I just . . . would you just . . . send me his email?"

Prof. Mark went scurrying out the door toward the elevator. Dave watched after him, puzzled, then leaned out the door to call down the hallway, "So, I can tell him you're interested?"

"Definitely!" Prof. Mark shouted, dashing into the elevator and pressing the button repeatedly.

"See you next Thursday!" Dave shouted back.

"I sure hope so," Prof. Mark replied. He tapped his foot impatiently. The closing elevator doors seemed to take forever, as did the slow descent to the ground floor. And even as he exited the hallway, his first glance of Atlanta's infamous rush-hour traffic through the glass doors took his breath away.

"Ughh," grunted Jackson, beholding the worried look on Prof. Mark's face. "Downtown traffic at this hour, am I right?"

"You have no idea how right you are," Prof. Mark agreed, feeling suddenly dizzy.

With an unsteady hand, he reached for the door.

He was really starting to worry what mayhem awaited him back home.

CHAPTER FIVE:
One Bad Idea Meets Its Maker

Traffic had not been kind to him, and the rain-slickened pavement added another half-hour to Prof. Mark's usual hour-long drive home from Midtown to the outskirts of Norcross, northeast of Atlanta. When he came up the stairs to their second-story landing, he almost tripped twice on his wet sneakers.

He jiggled the key, and the door opened. The apartment was surprisingly quiet . . . and completely dark. "Honey, I'm home," he said.

There was no reply.

This was *wrong*. Lisa should have beat him home by at least two hours.

He flicked the light switch, but nothing happened. He took a few steps forward, and in the gloom of the living room, he could barely make out what seemed like struggling forms piled onto the couch, chairs, and along the floor.

There was an eerie creak of hinges behind him, and the door slammed shut. "Deadbeat, is that you?" asked Prof. Mark, his concern growing. He thought he heard a muffled exclamation, and then the soft flapping of webbed feet on the linoleum in the kitchen beside him.

Next there was a soft *click*, and a table lamp lit inches away from him.

Prof. Mark stifled a gasp.

Almost on cue, a loud blast of thunder outside added stark, flickering illumination to a nightmarish visage before him.

Grinning at him with wild-colored, concentric-circle eyes was the half-lit face of Daggur Bill Platypus. Although he gave the credit to Dr. Ratnest for the character's creation, he knew all too well the crazed glare, the zigzagging spikes of hair, and worst of all, the jagged, saber-toothed grin that leered at him. These were the details he himself had first drawn during his internship nearly fifteen years before.

Daggur Bill was, after all, *his* design.

He never regretted making a single sketch so much in his life.

"Welcome home, Pro-fess-ofer," said Daggur Bill.

"You'll have to forgive me, but that linen closet was a little too limiting. And one thing we both have in common—neither of us can stand *limited* animation, can we?"

Bill shuddered with a cold, cruel chuckle before snapping his eyes wide open again at Prof. Mark. "I just needed a few moments to get out and stretch my . . . talents. I found your little Saturday morning friends didn't care much for my company, so I had to, well, incapacitate them. *Temporarily*, mind you, so don't you fret." Another cold chuckle followed. "Well . . . at least not . . . *just* yet. "

As Prof. Mark's eyes adjusted to the light, he could see that everyone—even his wife and pets—was tied and gagged.

"Well, I see your handiwork has taken care of everyone else here," he admitted. "Even down to tying up the parakeets, and a very thorough job of *that*, might I add. Though I hardly think even you could have taken care of Zhae-Garr, and—"

"Oh, guess again, Pro-fess-ofer," chuckled Bill. "All I had to do was place your open sketchbook in his path, and he went plummeting back inside. So, don't worry. Our proceedings won't be troubled by his distracting foot-quakes."

"Yeah, and—wait a minute." Prof. Mark's gaze searched the prisoners. "Where's Girth Grizzly? What have you done with him?"

"Oh, don't you go worrying about that goofball grizzly," answered Bill. "I wasn't about to harm a single hair from the accomplice in my escape. Well, at least not permanently . . ."

"Accomplice? Surely Girth wouldn't do something like let *you* out on purpose."

"Maybe not on *purpose*," Bill replied. "But I also have to thank my creator—the *other* one, naturally—for giving me the idea of who would help me escape. Eh, Ratnest? Remember? 'Neither I nor anyone here would be *foolish* enough to do such a thing.' Right, old pal?"

Dr. Ratnest, bound and gagged like all the others, could only grumble and narrow his eyes at his former lab assistant.

"So, that brings it down to you . . . and me, Pro-fess-ofer," said Daggur Bill. "What, oh whatever is to be done . . . with *you*?"

The psychopathic platypus edged closer to Prof. Mark, chuckling coldly.

***

Down atop a lonesome hill, Girth Grizzly was still sniffling.

Though he was technically back home in the sketch-book, just outside the rural town of Dixieville, he had never felt more homesick in his life. He missed his old friends, his new friends . . . and Prof. Mark.

All he really knew was that Daggur Bill had tricked him, and now all his friends, old and new, were in se-rious trouble. "And worst of all," muttered Girth, "it's all my fault. And I can't do nothin' about it!"

"Now, I wonder what could have a big fella like yourself in such a state," said a friendly voice that seemed to appear out of nowhere. "I've known you as long as I can recall, and I ain't never seen you so much as shed a tear."

Girth wiped his eyes and turned around. There, standing beside him, were his friends from the Dixieville jug band. There was Jughead Jethro, the tall, skinny banjo player, who had spoken. Standing even taller behind Jethro was a hulking harmonica player in sunglasses, Lil' Cornell Jr.

Below, Brer Jackalope, a fiddle-playing mountain hare with antlers, leaned lazily against the knee of Lil' Cornell Jr.

Girth had to look down to see the bearded accordion player Tall Clyde, at almost three feet tall.

Asleep on the ground beside him was Brer Bloodhound. From the dog's tail dangled Brer Possum in overalls and an oversized hat, snoring noisily.

Lil' Cornell Jr. stuck out a large, helpful hand and pulled Girth to his feet, then dusted him off. "There, now. Straighten up, and you tell us what's goin' on with ya."

"Well, fellas, it might seem hard to believe, but last night, Sezquatch, Deadbeat, and Thurman and me was sittin' right here by Deadbeat's trash barrel, like we usually do, when there was a blindin' flash of light. Next thing we knew, we was in this artist studio, and this feller named Prof. Mark there, he says he's the cartoonist that drew every one of us. And more cartoon characters kept poppin' out of his sketchbook, like this really purty bat lady named Jayle. I thought she'd taken a fancy to me, but it turned out to be this crazy platypus critter named Daggur Bill, who kicked me right back down here to Dixieville. Now Sezquatch, Deadbeat, Thurman, and those other nice folks are in danger from that crazy platypus, who's doin', well, who knows what to 'em!"

For a moment, Jughead Jethro and his friends found themselves dumbfounded.

Then they burst into laughter.

Just as Girth started to get angry, his dull yellow eyes beginning to redden, Jethro stopped laughing and waved his hands for the others to quiet down.

"Excuse me, big fella," said Tall Clyde, "but down here in Dixieville, we've heard some tall tales. I'll be danged if that one don't beat *anything* I ever done heard!"

"Now, hold on there, Tall Clyde," said Jethro.

"That's just the thing that gets me here. How long we all known Girth there?"

"Well, ever since he was a bear cub," yawned Brer Bloodhound, scratching his head with a hind leg.

"And now y'all mention it," said Brer Jackalope, "not *oncet* has I ever known him to fib."

Jughead Jethro stood in deep thought a moment, and looked up. "Well, don't that beat all you ever seen?" he exclaimed, his head aimed skyward as his arm pointed in the same direction. "You fellers ever seen anything the likes of *that*?"

The others looked up. On the other side of the fluffy clouds, floating what seemed like miles above, a jagged tear had appeared in the sky with edges that looked like torn paper.

"As farfetched as Girth's story sounds," explained Jethro, "I sure can't think of any *other* explanation for a tear in the sky. Can you fellers?"

After a muttered moment of confusion, followed by a round of head-scratching, the others had to admit they couldn't.

"Well, it sounds to me as though we're gonna have to figure out a way back up yonder and help those nice folks out," concluded Jughead Jethro. "But how?"

There was another extended, awkward round of head-scratching.

"If we just had some rope," suggested Lil' Cornell Jr., "we might could lasso it up and fasten it to somethin' on the other side."

"But where we gonna get some rope?" replied Tall Clyde.

Brer Possum yawned and offered a seemingly endless loop of rope from underneath his hat with a helpful, gap-toothed grin.

"Tarnation, if'n that possum don't have everything but the kitchen sank tucked up underneath that sombrero of his," muttered Tall Clyde.

Brer Possum grinned and held up a kitchen sink.

"I stand corrected," griped Tall Clyde.

"That's well enough, but I'm not sure even Lil' Cornell Jr. can lasso somethin' that high up," observed Jughead Jethro.

"Even if I could," said Lil' Cornell Jr., "there's no guarantee it'll catch on the other side."

"Only way we could make sure o' that is to fly it up. But you'd need wings for somethin' like that!" Tall Clyde crossed his arms. "And I doubt any of *us* is gonna sprout wings anytime soo—"

Tall Clyde was smacked to the ground by a feathered form, and both went rolling halfway down the hill before the others could help both the accordion player and the winged newcomer to their feet.

"Brer Turkey Buzzard!" shouted Tall Clyde. "Do you have any idea how tired I am of gettin' smacked senseless by your carrion-crawlin' carcass?"

"So s-s-sorry about that," stuttered the buzzard. "But I c-co-couldn't help noticin' what seemed sure to me the s-sw-sweet aroma of roadkill."

"Sorry to disappoint you, Brer Turkey Buzzard,"

Jughead Jethro said. "But that was probably just Brer Bloodhound again. You know he won't let us give him a bath!"

"Bath! Bath?" whimpered Brer Bloodhound, cowering behind Lil' Cornell Jr.

"Now, let's not start *that* routine again," Girth broke in. "Brer Turkey Buzzard, we need your help, and we need it fast! Can you carry a rope up to that zig-zaggety tear thing in the sky?"

Brer Turkey Buzzard eyed the target and nodded. "Hand me that there r-ro-rope, boys. I'll fetch it up there for ya!"

With a resounding cheer from the jug band and their animal friends, they fastened the rope around the buzzard's waist and made ready for their skyward journey back to the artist studio.

CHAPTER SIX:
Saturday Morning Mayhem!

Back in the apartment, Daggur Bill seemed to be enjoying his impending capture of Prof. Mark. He finally had his creator backed into a corner—literally.

The cartoonist looked around, not seeing any escape, and expected the worst from his saber-toothed captor.

"The only thing that really upset me about my capture by such a worthless band of Saturday morning rejects," said Daggur Bill as he inched closer, "was that you somehow managed to separate me from that one sacred object without which I feel . . . oh, *almost* helpless. My dear, sweet axe. Unspeakable," he sneered. "How could you ever hide my Unspeakable Axe in such a small apartment?"

"At least we managed to—" Prof. Mark began, but with a quick *swish*, Daggur Bill brought out the notched weapon from under his shirt.

"Whoops! Found it!" chuckled the grimacing platypus. "Always the *last* darn place you look, ain't it?"

Prof. Mark's head sank as he watched Daggur Bill lower the axe to one of his poison spurs and run it along the drop of venom oozing out.

"Now . . . where were we?" Bill turned back toward Prof. Mark. "Ah, yes. Your impending demise. Got it."

Prof. Mark exchanged a glance with his wife, still

struggling from her confines on the couch. "Aw, honey . . . everybody, I'm so sorry. This is all my fault. When I let my imagination run wild, I . . ."

He paused when he saw Girth peering around the corner, a cautious finger to his lips. Prof. Mark nodded grimly to himself, and then at the platypus.

"I almost let it get the best of me sometimes. *Almost.*" He muttered, "I guess it took *brawn* to let brains like yours out, Daggur Bill."

"What?" sneered Daggur Bill. "What exactly do you mean, Pro-fess-ofer?"

Prof. Mark looked away, trying not to draw the villain's attention to the creeping forms gathering behind him in the hallway. "Well, it's just ironic that, as smart as you *consider* yourself, you'd still be locked inside that closet had it not been for someone, well . . . *slightly* less of an intellectual than yourself."

"Slightly?" snickered Daggur Bill. "*Slightly* less intelligent . . . than myself?"

"Well, yes, slightly. Um, *somewhat,*" added Prof. Mark.

"You have the audacity to insinuate," snarled Daggur Bill, "that Girth Grizzly bear of yours is *merely* slightly, or even somewhat, less intelligent than me?"

Daggur Bill didn't see it, but Girth Grizzly's eyes popped open wider at the mention of his name.

"Well, I did say *slightly,*" Prof. Mark agreed.

"And you call yourself a professor," chuckled Daggur Bill. "If you were any kind of intellectual yourself, you'd see that I'm twice—ho-ho-oh—no, *exponentially* smarter than that hairy oaf of yours!"

"Oaf? It's hardly fair to start calling anyone names, Daggur Bill. Girth has many redeeming qualities, and—"

"And not *one* of them can remotely be qualified as intelligence," Daggur Bill retorted. "That Girth Grizzly of yours has got to be the most gullible, dimwitted oaf who is without doubt the most st—"

"Don't you *dare* call any of my characters stupid, Daggur Bill," warned Prof. Mark.

"Stupid?" laughed Daggur Bill. "Stupid? It would be a *compliment* for me to call that stupid bear *stupid*!"

The room began to tremble, and for a moment, all began to think that somehow Zhae-Garr had returned from the sketchbook. Then it became clear the sound was a low growl, slowly growing to a roar—the roar of an enraged grizzly bear.

"If you can't call someone somethin' nice," said Girth Grizzly as he swelled with rage, "don't call 'em nothin' at all!"

Daggur Bill spun around to see Girth Grizzly with a club raised over his head. Every jagged quill on his head sagged. "Oh, no."

"Let me get one thing straight here," growled Girth as he knocked Daggur Bill's axe away with a single swipe of his club. "These folks are *my* friends, and I ain't about to let any no-account, dime-store villain like *you* do nothin' to harm 'em!" He snarled and took a step farther.

"Now, just— just a minute, Grizzly," Daggur Bill

muttered, backing into the same corner Prof. Mark had been trapped in. The platypus eyed the cartoonist angrily as he stepped aside. "If I'm a villain, it's because *he* drew me a villain! It's all his fault! I had a decent government job, and he and that whacked-out scientist *made* me this way! Blame him!"

"Well, Dr. Ratnest may have started out as a villain," Prof. Mark interrupted, pulling the gag away from the scientist's mouth as he spoke, "but ever since he got here, he's done nothing but try to help us!"

"Bill, I knew right away this world brought us here for a reason," stated Dr. Ratnest flatly. "We were brought here because we were *needed* here. It's certainly not perfect—at least no more so than that cartoon sketchbook we left behind—but while Prof. Mark may indeed have created us with character flaws, it's what gives us *personality*. And with it, each of us is driven by a personal desire to make whichever world we're brought to a better place than we found it!"

"*Yecch*. The world of bleeding hearts," scoffed the Platypus. "Spare me, you whiny little sons of a sketchbook! While I may not have my beloved axe, you all seem to have forgotten not one, but two tiny little details. Girth's shoes are untied."

"Oh, not again." Girth looked down. "I could've sworn—"

With a whirling motion only possible for a deranged cartoon character, Daggur Bill swirled around behind the bear and put Girth in a headlock. And although far smaller than the oversized grizzly, the metallic switchblade sound of Bill's poisonous platypus spur stopped less than an inch from Girth's throat.

Girth froze, wisely.

"Could've sworn you didn't *wear* shoes? Is *that* what you were about to say?" chuckled Daggur Bill. "Well, Girth, my shaggy, oversized oaf, since we all seem to agree intelligence isn't your strong point, let me let *you* in on a little secret." The platypus's eyes rolled toward his extended spur beneath Girth's neck.

"Even in this world, poison from the male platypus spur is one of the most painful injections a human can receive without being lethal," the platypus informed him. "The pain goes on for weeks, sometimes *months*. And while to such a big, strapping fella like yourself"—Daggur Bill smacked Girth's fuzzy cheek for emphasis—"I doubt it would be *lethal*. . . However, thanks to Dr. Ratnest's modification-uns to my physique, my spurs just might prove your very *painful* demise. What say we find out? Hmm?"

"Can I say one . . ." Girth mumbled, but Bill's headlock made it almost impossible to talk.

"Ughhh," groaned Bill. "What now, you oaf? What are *your* famous last words?" He rolled his eyes toward his confined crowd. "*This* oughta be good folks."

Girth coughed, and strained to speak. "Well, yeah, Prof. Mark may not have made me too smart, but he made me *strong*. And at least he gave me enough good sense to choose between right and wrong. I may have messed things up last time, but, well, this time *I'm* the one that's right . . . and you're wrong!" He coughed. "It was *your* shoes that was untied."

"No, you idiot, I don't even—" Daggur Bill looked down, and with that moment of distraction, Girth yanked the platypus' grip away before the deadly spur could flick closer to his throat. The two spun around in a violent whirlwind in a scene straight out of a Saturday morning cartoon.

It was impossible to see who was winning. Prof. Mark, Lisa, and all the confined characters could only look on helplessly, waiting for the outcome.

When the dust cleared, Girth's fingers were locked around the maniacal platypus's throat. Both of Daggur Bill's extended spurs kicked helplessly in midair as he fought to loosen the grizzly's grip.

"Gark! Mnf!" sputtered Bill. "Air . . . need . . . would be . . . *gulk* . . . nice!"

"I'm sorry, Bill, but we ain't gonna be able to let you stay conscious for your capture," Girth said. "You was right, you're mighty clever. You *just* might outsmart us again, so we can't take no chances." He tapped the platypus' head, indicating his intention. "We're just gonna have to knock you senseless!"

Daggur Bill's crazed eyes went even wider, and he stifled a whimper.

"Let's get 'em, fellers!" cried Jughead Jethro, appearing from around the hallway corner and waving a garden rake at the now-surrounded villain.

Jethro had hardly spoken when Girth's club came whistling down onto Daggur Bill's noggin.

The dazed platypus paused briefly, then, attempting to shake it off, snarled, "It's gonna take *wayyy* more than that to stop Daggur Bill Platypus, you Saturday morning simpletons!"

"No sooner s-sa-said than done," exclaimed Brer Turkey Buzzard, who began spinning around Bill with the rope. Lil' Cornell Jr. pulled it tight. The buzzard launched Bill into the air while the other members of the jug band, armed with their garden tools, stood around him in a circle below. "Anybody wanna play p-pi-piñata?" offered the buzzard.

"Me first!" shouted Lil' Cornell Jr., taking a whack at the platypus with a shovel.

"Hey, knock it off, ya country bump—" A garden hoe to Bill's beak interrupted him.

"I'm startin' to thank there ain't no candy inside this here ugly platypus piñata," griped Tall Clyde, who had landed the blow.

Brer Possum and Brer Bloodhound had already set about freeing the cartoon captives from their ropes and gags. All the characters were searching for makeshift clubs so they could join in the party game.

"Okay, that's enough, fellas," interrupted Prof. Mark. "I don't like to see any of my characters, even a lowlife like Daggur Bill, get permanently . . . damaged."

There was one last, loud *clunk* as Daggur Bill's head collided with a mop.

"*Clunk?* From a mop?" exclaimed Sezquatch. "How does a mop go *clunk*?"

"Easy," said Lisa, shaking the mop. "You just have to wrap an iron inside." The iron fell onto the ground with another *clunk*, landing on Deadbeat's toe. The skunk started hopping around wildly. "Sorry, Deadbeat," she apologized.

Deadbeat winced. "That's okay, Mrs. T." He added a wink. "I gotta admit, though, I like your style."

"All right, I think that just about wraps things up, Bill," said Prof. Mark, after he quickly hugged his wife. "Lousy pun intended."

"I got out of that linen closet *once*, Pro-fess-ofer," growled Daggur Bill, "and I'll do it *again*."

"Oh, we're not sending you back to the linen closet, Daggur Bill," Prof. Mark corrected him. "I think we're gonna send you back somewhere you can't hurt me or my family . . . of cartoon friends."

Daggur Bill's circled eyes widened in terror at the sight of the sketchbook being positioned by the professor in the hallway.

"No, not that sketchbook!" shrieked the platypus. "You wouldn't dare! The one with all those singing chipmunks, dancing flowers, and—"

"Girth, how would *you* like to play piñata?" suggested Lil' Cornell Jr. "I think you got a mighty fine whompin' stick handy."

Girth took grip of his large, thorned club and aimed toward the open sketchbook. "One . . . two . . ."

"No, don't," pleaded Daggur Bill. "Maybe we could work somethin' out. Maybe if you just erased my tusks, I could be nicer again and resume my career as a certified public accountant for the IRS, or—"

"Five . . . three!" Girth's club plowed through the air

and connected with the platypus' backside, sending the villain sailing down into the tear.

Prof. Mark picked the sketchbook up and placed a small strip of artist's tape over the rip. "That will hold him until Dr. Ratnest and I figure out how to handle this gateway matter." He gave a satisfied nod to the applause of all the characters in the apartment. "Girth, you did good," Prof. Mark said. "I couldn't be any prouder of *any* of my sketches, as if you were my own son."

Girth blushed while Jayle and all the other characters patted him on the back, taking turns to shake his paws and hug him like an oversized teddy bear.

"But in the meantime, won't Daggur Bill cause more trouble inside your sketchbook?" asked Lisa. "I mean, aren't the characters on the other side in danger from *him*?"

"Something tells me there's another character waiting over there that's going to keep Daggur Bill in check like never before," said Prof. Mark.

"Who's that, Prof. Mark?" asked Thurman.

"Well, isn't it obvious?" Prof. Mark slid his hands into his pockets with a smug grin. "He made an enemy *far* more dangerous than himself. And since I think cartoon comeuppance is the best variety, that's exactly what Daggur Bill is *about* to get."

CHAPTER SEVEN:
Cartoon Comeuppance

Far, far below the apartment, on a high hill in a cartoon meadow, beside a grizzly-shaped dent in the ground, a scowling platypus stood, his wild eyes fixed grimly upward.

"If those ridicu-lif-erous idiots up there think they can keep *me*, Daggur Bill Platypus, prisoner in this sappy Saturday morning sketchbook, they've got another think coming," grumbled the platypus, swinging a rope with a grappling hook on the loose end. He eyed the tattered tear in the sky, certain of his aim. "No, sirree, you can't keep a bad platypu—"

"*Platypus!* Daggur Bill *Platypus*?" growled a voice that shook the very ground beneath his webbed feet.

Bill gulped. That was something he didn't do often—well, actually, *ever*. His concentric-circled eyes blinked warily as he turned around.

What he thought before had been two twin hills were drifting toward him through the cartoon mist of the dark evening. The hills were actually the shadowy, shaggy shoulders of the massive giant Zhae-Garr. At the base of the two mountains, two yellow-green eyes, each the size of a tractor tire, glared down at him.

"So, you thought you could trap Zhae-Garr in this odd world of outlined trees and singing butterflies without *retribution*, did you?"

Daggur Bill backed away, but was blocked by a massive fist of clawed fingers. It was like being trapped in the center of an uprooted redwood. "Hey, big guy, back off, will ya?" Bill was thoroughly unfamiliar with having to back down to anyone himself. He didn't like it, but . . . he had no choice. "I'm on your side, right? C'mon, let's get back up there and show those goody-goodies who's boss, huh? Whaddya say?"

"Zhae-Garr has no *boss* in this world," bellowed the giant. "Zhae-Garr is about to play a game with this diminutive duckbill who thinks his whimpering schemes can fool a giant older than the mountains I am often mistaken for! But fear not, you cowering cretin, for Zhae-Garr likes his sport. And so, I shall give you . . . a head start."

"Well, at least that's someth—" Bill started to say, but winced in pain. The giant's large claws had formed a viselike grip

against the platypus' beaver tail as he pulled back, while the other massive paw pinched Daggur Bill's midsection in place.

"Um, big guy, that more than just *kinda* hurts, and I'm hardly in what you would call a bargaining position here, mind you. So, I'm not sure if maybe there's some *other* way we could handle this awkward situa—ow, OW, OW!"

Bill didn't like where this was going. He had seen this on the other cartoons in Prof. Mark's sketchbook.

Zhae-Garr was playing "slingshot" with his body and tail.

Bill grimaced. "Oh, no."

The giant released Bill's tail, which had been pulled so tight, the platypus thought it was about to come off. With a resounding *snap*, his tail popped against his seat, and thanks to the exaggerated laws of cartoon physics, Daggur Bill went sailing through the clouds over the misty hills on the outlined horizon.

"Don't thank me *yet*, you ugly duckbill," Zhae-Garr growled, "for though I am older and taller than the hills, my senses are acute. And yes, I will find you—no matter how many *pieces* you land in."

With a chuckle colder than even Daggur Bill's, Zhae-Garr shifted his mighty weight and started off toward the distant platypus.

CHAPTER EIGHT:
One Big, Happy Cartoon Family

Sezquatch cleared away the dishes as Prof. Mark, Lisa, and the rest of their new cartoon roommates wiped their mouths (most with napkins, but a few with paws and furry wrists), patting their bellies contentedly.

"Sezquatch, you outdid yourself with that breakfast," Lisa sighed.

"It's just nice to be appreciated for your talents, Mrs. Toonery," the grinning, orange bigfoot said, heading for the kitchen. "Thurman, you wanna help me with these dishes?"

"Sure thing," the porcupine agreed. "Which reminds me!" He stood up in his chair, waving for attention. "Okay, everybody, don't forget to check this week's chore list after we clean up the dishes. I want this apartment shipshape when the Toonerys get back from work tonight. Right, guys?"

Deadbeat and Marty the Gargoyle scrambled over to the refrigerator, examining the chart.

"Oh, good," sighed the gargoyle. "Thurman's got himself doin' the laundry again, and I get . . . yes! DVD organization! That rocks!"

As the gargoyle went through a series of poses better reserved for a touchdown, Deadbeat took one look at the chart and his face fell. "I can't believe I gotta walk these dogs every day," he grumbled. "I mean, it's not that I mind helpin' around the house, but . . . Ratnest, do you think you could come up with some sort of device to, well, take care of such *unsightly* matters?"

The lab rat shook his head, waving his hand at the skunk's request. "Sorry, young fellow, I have more immediate and *urgent* matters on which to focus my attentions." Dr. Ratnest sauntered into the hallway to stand beside an oversized Y-switch on the wall by the linen closet. "Observe, if you will, everyone."

The scientist flipped the switch into place and a large, metal-paneled door snapped shut horizontally, followed by a second pair of vertical doors. Steam hissed and a red light flashed over the spot that had once been the linen closet. "There, that should contain that rip in your sketchbook until we can figure out how to handle this doorway between our worlds, Prof. Mark."

"Thank you, Dr. Ratnest," Prof. Mark said. "That handles the two most dangerous characters. But what about—"

"The rest of us oddballs?" said Marty the Gargoyle. "I was kinda wondering about that myself."

Petrol stepped forward. "Well, Prof. Mark, as you know, I've always had trouble keeping your Arsonist Space Squirrels in line. I figured we'd find a more socially acceptable outlet for their . . . special talents, at least in *this* world."

"Cirque du Solaris?" asked Krispy.

"Kindergarten teachers?" offered Krunchy.

"The National Guard," Petrol Jelly corrected both squirrels. "There are a lot of civilians in this world who could use our protection."

"Well, at my work, they've said we could use some extra help," said Lisa. "And Jayle tells me she can type two hundred twenty-five words per minute. That kind of cartoon speed will be especially appreciated in this world. And I really appreciate all of you helping around the apartment—Sezquatch cooking, Deadbeat walking the dogs, and . . ."

"But what about the rest of us?" asked Thurman. "You're not going to send *us* back into the sketchbook, are you, Mrs. Toonery?" The porcupine gazed at Prof. Mark's wife with moist, glistening eyes.

Dr. Ratnest stepped forward. "I don't think there will be any need for such teary farewells, my quill-en-crusted companion. Prof. Mark also asked me to take over his new Cartoonyville.com website, and whilst I was reading his email, I found a couple of items that will be of interest . . . to us all. It led to *this* envelope, the contents of which I will share with you directly." He wagged a folded letter with a paperclip.

"Will you please read it, then, Dr. Ratnest?" requested Lisa.

"Gladly, dear lady," replied Dr. Ratnest with a genuine smile, clearing his throat and unfolding the printed letter. "'Dear Prof. Mark, it is with great eagerness we read your proposal for a book about how to make cartoons, so we will gladly publish your title *The Art of Flash Animation: Creative Cartooning*. Please find enclosed an advance check for the amount of . . .' Oh dear, could this be a typo? Aha, now I understand. It continues, 'And furthermore, upon our advisement by one Dave Friendly, animation director of our sister company in televised entertainment, Atlanta's cable network, the Atlantamation Sta—"

"Atlanta?" exclaimed Deadbeat. "Is that where we are now?"

Thurman's eyes popped open with shimmering cartoon stars. "Why, that's like . . . the Hollywood of the South!"

"If I *may* continue," grumbled Dr. Ratnest with a sneer. "'This station, noted in the attachment below, is interested in the lovable characters you used to illustrate your book—Deadbeat Skunk, Thurman Q. Porcupine, etc.—starring on your proposed cable show regarding a cartoonist sharing his two-bedroom apartment with a group of his own wacky cartoon characters, who recently escaped his sketchbook.'"

Dr. Ratnest paused to exchange a knowing grin with Prof. Mark. "Well, well, wherever *do* you come up with these farfetched cartoon ideas, Prof. Mark?"

Lisa took the check from Dr. Ratnest and eyed it in disbelief. "Well, everyone, I think this may be the time for an announcement of my own. We're going to need a bigger place to live."

"But, honey," Prof. Mark interrupted, "three characters just announced they're about to leave. Jayle has a job to help out with the bills . . . that's three incomes. So, why do we need a bigger place if we have *fewer* characters?"

"Because I want a house with a fenced-in backyard for a *new* character to play in."

"A new character?" asked Prof. Mark, confused.

"Her name will be Stacey Toonery . . . and she'll be arriving in about five months," said Lisa, patting her belly. "Isn't that great news, dear? . . . Dear?"

Lisa looked down beside her.

Prof. Mark had fainted.

"I'll get the smelling salts," said Deadbeat, "and while I'm at it, I guess I'll look around for another leash, if I'm gonna be expected to walk that *baby*, too."

After assisting Prof. Mark back to his feet, the other characters shuffled over to view the impending tasks on the chore list. Jayle stepped away from the group and quietly motioned for Girth to approach her. Girth looked to either side, confused, then pointed to himself bashfully.

Jayle nodded, smiling sweetly, and Girth took a step forward to her.

"Hey, Girth," Jayle said, rocking on her bare heels. "Thurman told me about how Daggur Bill tricked you, and even though I didn't know *anything* about it at the time, I just wanted to say I'm sorry . . . and that I thought it was, well, really sweet of you to try to rescue me from that linen closet, even though, y'know, I was never *actually* trapped in there."

"Well, gosh, Miss Jayle, I just don't know what to say. I'm not very good with words, or, well, anything when it comes to . . . *thinkin'* stuff, y'know."

"Well, then, leave it to me, Girth," said Jayle warmly.

"Thank you for *trying* to rescue me." She leaned over and gave him a quick kiss on his fuzzy cheek.

Girth's eyes popped open wide, and with the sound of a boiling kettle, he shuddered and leaped into the air, cartoon fireworks exploding all around him. "Yee-*haww*!" he shouted.

Deadbeat and Marty the Gargoyle exchanged glances of awe and disbelief.

"Well, if that don't beat all," muttered Deadbeat. "I was sure I had a chance at her."

"Me, too." Marty sighed wearily. He whipped out something that almost looked like a racing form from his furry loincloth pocket. Dabbing a pencil against his tongue, he traced a pathway down a long column of figures. "So, who won the pool in 'Who smooches Jayle first?'"

Prof. Mark held his hand out expectantly. "Right here, fellas. Pay up."

"Prof. *Mark*?" exclaimed the skunk and the gargoyle together.

"B-buh-but how—?" sputtered Deadbeat.

"Hey, don't act so surprised, fellas. I'm not just an animator, I'm a *cartoonist*. I *write* all this stuff, too, remember?"

EPILOGUE:
Fleece and Fake Fur

Dr. Ratnest leaned forward from the apartment hallway, his gloved hand against the corner, and looked side to side, then outward. The scientist scanned the living room and spotted Prof. Mark. Clearing his throat for the cartoonist's attention, he gave Prof. Mark an ominous nod. Dr. Ratnest motioned his creator over to the hallway. The cartoonist, looking concerned, followed.

Dr. Ratnest looked around, making sure no one was listening. Convinced they would be alone, the scientist walked into the hallway. "Prof. Mark, a private word with you, if I may?"

Catching up to the scientist, Prof. Mark followed him toward the studio. "What's wrong, Dr. Ratnest?"

Dr. Ratnest gestured grandly toward his metallic safety doors over the linen closet. "Well, having contained the breach between our two worlds, for the moment, it seems, on *that* point, all seems to be well. However . . ."

"However . . .?" asked Prof. Mark.

"Yes, there is indeed, regrettably, a *however*." Dr. Ratnest led Prof. Mark over to the studio art desk and leaned down, motioning to a box taped shut. "However, while I secured your sketchbook, I noticed there was another box beside it also marked for storage, which seemed a bit, well, *lively*."

"Not more free-roaming cartoon characters, I hope?" Prof. Mark groaned.

"Oh, no," Dr. Ratnest assured him, reluctantly tapping his index fingers together. "No more . . . *cartoon* characters."

"Well, I hope you don't mean a pest problem, like we've got ra—ra . . ."

The oversized lab rat raised a warning eyebrow, and Prof. Mark quickly caught himself to avoid insulting the scientist.

"*Mice,* not like mice or anything." Prof. Mark cleared his throat awkwardly.

"No, not cartoons," said Dr. Ratnest, gritting his teeth, "and not *mice.*"

"Well, if not cartoons or mice, that doesn't really leave much, except . . ." Prof. Mark's eyes followed Ratnest's hand, which pointed downward to the cardboard box.

The scientist leaned down and drummed his gloved fingers on the box in question. At his contact, the box began struggling with a muffled noise like a bunch of squeaky dog toys. Dr. Ratnest nodded at the box. "Well, I had a rather interesting conversation with your charming wife earlier. She tells me before you began seriously considering *cartooning* as a career, *before* you wanted to be a writer, even, you built . . ."

Ratnest ripped off the packing tape and the box burst open. The room was filled with hopping little shadows and mischievous giggling figures.

Prof. Mark shielded his eyes with both hands, leaning backward. "Puppets!"

A shadow with moose antlers rose out of the box above all the other wriggling fleece and fake-fur figures. It shook itself, as though prematurely awakened from a nap, and glared condescendingly at the scowling scientist.

"And just who are you supposed to be?" demanded Dr. Ratnest.

The moose puppet, wearing a space uniform, dusted himself off and placed his hand to his hip, the other gloved hand saluting.

Dr. Ratnest and Prof. Mark both backed away to the wall, not quite knowing what to expect.

"I'm Admiral Zap Antler . . . of the Cosmoose!" he announced.

"I don't suppose either of you have seen a couple of Arsonist Space Squirrels running around anywhere, have you?"

THE END

I certainly hope you enjoyed this first installation of my planned trilogy enough to look forward to the remaining stories. While a far cry from epic tales like those of Tolkien and C. S. Lewis (that I grew up on, along with the wonderful worlds of Jim Henson, Bob Keeshan's *Captain Kangaroo*, *Mister Rogers' Neighborhood*, Hanna-Barbera, Sid and Marty Krofft), I think you'll enjoy the continued adventures as Dr. Ratnest and Prof. Mark manage the interdimensional breach between the second and third dimensions.

The Cartoonyville Halloween Caper
Dr. Ratnest perfects the gateway between worlds and works with Prof. Mark to open an interdimensional theme park, Cartoonyville! Visitors can now travel to a cartoon adventure park populated by living cartoon characters and divided into four sections: Dixieville, Jungleville, Fairybookville, and Videoville.

Prof. Mark and his cartoon buddies Deadbeat Skunk and Thurman are about to welcome everyone to the grand opening on Halloween, when their video greeting is interrupted by a strange laser beam. After blinking their shielded eyes, they realize Deadbeat's outline has disappeared—worse yet, he's been turned into a puppet!

Soon the strange beam returns, and all over the park

cartoon employees and human visitors alike are being turned into puppets. Prof. Mark sends Park Ranger Ray-Ray and her puppet sidekick, Dimentrodon Dinosaur, to investigate some mysterious lights from an abandoned hotel in Jungleville to see if there's a connection to the transformations.

Cartoonyville Dark Ride

Nine years after opening Cartoonyville, the novelty of living cartoon characters has worn off with the public, and park attendance has dropped off considerably. Worse yet, an accident has faced Prof. Mark with a lawsuit that threatens to close the park permanently.

Prof. Mark turns to the combined efforts of Dr. Ratnest and his own daughter to come up with a new ride to renew teen interest in the park while settling the legal issues. The two collaborate with two other teen cartoons—a bat named Jayle and Marty the Gargoyle—to design a dark ride based on Dr. Ratnest's own Haunted Castle.

Most goes well, until reports from trial runs of the new attraction come back describing a fanged platypus attacking the riders. Could Daggur Bill Platypus have returned from the cartoon grave to haunt the dark ride? Or has Dr. Ratnest himself, the supposedly reformed mad scientist, secretly renewed his own twisted experiments that somehow brought back his old lab assistant?

Thanks so much for reading! As an additional thank-you, here's an excerpt from the next story in the Cartoonyville Trilogy.

THE CARTOONYVILLE HALLOWEEN CAPER:
Opening Night

Prof. Mark stood watching the crowds in the video studio as they prepared their first television special. The occasion was Halloween, and it also happened to be the animator's birthday. The cartoon auditorium beyond the stage lights housed at least three hundred hand-drawn seats occupied by mixed crowds of human guests, a few celebrities who resided in the greater Atlanta area, and cartoon staff, along with a few living puppets who strained their plastic eyes, some standing on each other's shoulders to see over the taller guests seated in front of them.

The cartoon professor nodded to a question he barely heard as a human sound engineer stepped away. He guessed it had been something about a mic check, but he was obviously distracted among all the hushed conversations that were dying down as the broadcast debut drew nearer. Prof. Mark had declined the suggestion to wear a suit and tie, and instead stood in his trademark blue-striped shirt and cyan ballcap, though he had at least opted for black denim jeans instead of his preferred blue. He stood rocking on his sneakered heels, uncharacteristically nervous.

"Boss, calm down, already," sighed Deadbeat Skunk,

his cartoon sidekick. Deadbeat crossed his arms and rolled his eyes sideways at the artist who had first drawn him nearly twenty years ago. "Everything's gonna go just fine. You *got* this. What's the worst that could happen?"

"We've invited almost two thousand humans from the third dimension—through Dr. Ratnest's experimental interdimensional gateway, no less—here into one of my old sketchbooks," Prof. Mark replied with a huff. "Plenty could go wrong. The gateway could shut down, trapping us here permanently . . . I mean, I've gone through this plenty of times, but what if we or one of these guests gets maimed by another one of my fantasy illustrations on a rampage?"

"Relax, pal," said Deadbeat. "We've explored this sketchbook a hundred times. You know every sketch in here like the back of your hand. Besides, when have you *ever* known one of Dr. Ratnest's gizmos to fail?"

"Like, *never*," interrupted Thurman, the blue-quilled porcupine. "That guy's a genius. He knows what he's doing!"

"I just wish he could've made it. I'd sure feel better if he were here. I mean, this whole cartoon amusement park wouldn't be possible without him. I'm surprised he passed up the appreciation of the opening-day crowd. It's a little out of character, actually . . ."

"With all due respect, Prof. Mark," said Thurman shyly, "the poor guy was on the verge of a nervous breakdown. Overseeing the rides, inspecting and reinspecting the integrity of that interdimensional bridge, um . . . thingy . . ."

"And you wouldn't want another one of your cartoon characters to go over the edge," advised Deadbeat. "Seeing *one* of your drawings as a psychopath was enough for three hand-drawn lifetimes," he grumbled.

"Six," added Thurman with a shudder, referring to the fateful night nearly five years ago when they first popped out of their sketchbook into Prof. Mark's studio. They had been followed by ten more of Prof. Mark's sketches, including a psychopathic platypus with walrus-like tusks: a fiend named Daggur Bill. The distraction of a gigantic monster emerging from Prof. Mark's unpublished fantasy illustrations, a shaggy titan named Zhae-Garr, had provided enough opportunity for the other characters to overpower the platypus, and much later, with the help of the giant, eventually his riddance.

"There's just so much we don't know about human and cartoon interaction. What if someone gets bitten by a cartoon mosquito? Will they turn *into* a cartoon, um, mosquito?" Prof. Mark rubbed the back of his neck.

"Boss, really, settle down. Mosquitoes aren't vampires—well, not *actually*. Besides, I've never even seen you draw a mosquito here! So, I doubt that's a genuine concern. Look around at all these people. They've dreamed of meeting actual cartoon characters their whole lives! Not some sweaty college kids in fur suits trying to earn extra bucks on their spring break down in Florida. You and Dr. Ratnest have opened the gateway to a *real* cartoon world for *your* whole world to enjoy. So, take a cue from your fans, Prof. Mark. Settle back and enjoy yourself for once!"

"He's right, y'know," Thurman agreed. "You're not a struggling cartoonist anymore. We're here for you!"

Prof. Mark sighed and nodded as his two cartoon friends patted his back. He looked over at his wife, Lisa, and his young daughter, Stacey Toonery, standing just out of range of the video lights. They simultaneously blew kisses to him.

They must have rehearsed that, he thought with a bemused smile. He was going to have to spend more time with those two once this pilot episode was done. "Okay, you're right. My family and friends are here to support me," said Prof. Mark. "Let's do this."

Deadbeat nodded to the cartoon camera operator, a hulking reptile named Goshzilla. He tapped the red button, and the oversized video-camera monitors lining the studio were emblazoned with captions reading, LIVE RECORDING.

"We're rolling!" exclaimed Goshzilla.

The crowd responded with all the noise expected of a cartoon zoo as they jumped up and down wildly.

The animated credits rolled on the monitors.

Cartoonyville Studios was officially open.

"I mean, I don't know why you guys are so worried," muttered Thurman as everyone shuffled to their positions. "Seriously, I've seen cartoons and humans interact *all* the time. Like, well, what about that cartoon rabbit thingy and the detective? Or was that a jackalope? And that English nanny who went into that sidewalk-chalk drawing?" He leaned forward in his seat, scratching his blue quills as Goshzilla flipped on the QUIET sign for the studio audience.

"Those were just *movies*, buddy." Deadbeat blinked at the porcupine.

"Oh, yeah . . ."

"Shh," warned Prof. Mark. "The opening credits are almost done."

"And we are live in three, two . . ." grunted Goshzilla in his gravelly voice. He pointed at them, and Prof. Mark began his video welcome.

"Howdy, thrillseekers," he announced, and the studio applauded. "I'm Prof. Mark Toonery, welcoming you to Cartoonyville with my good buddies Thurman Q. Porcupine and Deadbeat Skunk."

"What's going on in Cartoonyville today, Prof. Mark?" Thurman asked, reading the cue cards held by Jayle, an attractive, large-eared female bat with tangerine skin and oversized headphones, one of the other original crew from Prof. Mark's apartment.

"I'm glad you asked, Thurman, because today's a very special—"

A bright, flickering beam blasted from one of the spotlights mounted on the balcony, and a shadowy figure aimed it at Deadbeat, who shuddered and began making involuntary jabbering sounds. It lasted only a moment, but to everyone else, it seemed longer. The light intensified until the whole room was warmed in a blaze of extended lightning. Then, without warning, every light in the studio went out. Only the light from individual cell phones in the audience provided pockets of illumination among the disbelieving faces of the studio guests.

"Hey, the lights are off! What's happening?" bellowed Goshzilla into his headset.

"Can you get that backup generator running for me, Marty?" shouted Jayle. A green-winged gargoyle obliged, throwing the large Y-switch that Dr. Ratnest had installed for emergencies.

Almost immediately, the lights returned, and those on the set looked around in confusion.

At first glance, everyone seemed okay, even Deadbeat, although their eyes were still adjusting to the previous flicker of lights and the unexplained spotlight effect.

"Let's pick up where we left off," suggested Goshzilla, and he cued the trio in front of the camera.

"What was that about? And Deadbeat—" Prof. Mark stammered, looking at his cartoon friend as his eyes focused on the skunk. His outline was gone, and his shiny black-and-white cartoon fur had changed into plush fake fur! His eyes, instead of shifting back and forth characteristically, were now plastic, with small felt pupils aimed dead ahead in a fixed stare, his purple eyelids now permanently at half-mast.

"Deadbeat, what happened?" Prof. Mark looked up and down disbelievingly.

"I don't know. I feel strange. I—hey, wait a minute!" Deadbeat looked fearfully at his arms. "What happened to my outline?"

"Deadbeat, you've been changed into a . . . a puppet!" gasped Prof. Mark.

The audience murmured. *Was this part of the show?*

"Something extra weird is definitely going on in Cartoonyville," Thurman said. "It can only mean one thing . . ."

"What's that?" asked the Deadbeat puppet.

"It means this is . . . *The Cartoonyville Halloween Caper*!" Thurman waved his arms and began screaming uncontrollably, and ran off set.

With a frenzied waving motion, Goshzilla signaled them to stop. "Um, uh . . . cue commercial!" he nervously announced.

***

Jayle, Marty the Gargoyle, and Goshzilla rushed up to Prof. Mark and the Deadbeat puppet. Goshzilla picked up Thurman from his panicked run, and winced at the quilled tail in his grasp.

"Wow, great special effects!" exclaimed Marty, looking up and down the skunk. "I didn't think we had anything like *that* in the show budget." He plucked at one of Deadbeat's arms, which the skunk yanked back.

"It's not a special effect, doofus!" retorted Jayle, smacking Marty on the back of his head.

"Quiet, you guys," said Prof. Mark. "We gotta figure out what's going on here, and quick. This show is live, and maybe for the moment it might be better if the audience thinks it *was* a publicity gimmick. If everybody thinks the park isn't safe—"

"Yeah, we can't afford for this place to get shut

down," agreed the Deadbeat puppet. "Loss of the T-shirt sales alone . . . I've got *merchandising* deals to think of, people!"

"We've only got a three-minute commercial break here," grumbled Prof. Mark. "Okay, first things first. Who was working that spotlight up there?"

"New guy," Jayle answered, her graceful bat wings twitching fitfully from her elbows. She gazed up at the spotlight, now abandoned. "Kind of a creepy character, come to think of it."

"Was it a cartoon or a puppet?" asked Prof. Mark.

"Hard to say. He was wearing a trench coat and sunglasses, now that you mention it. Almost like he didn't want us to see who he was."

"Trench coats are never good news," mumbled Deadbeat. "How did he get through security?"

"Jayle, see if you can locate Ratnest and get him in here to help Deadbeat," said Prof. Mark. "If you can't find him, contact Petrol Jelly and the Arsonist Space Squirrels, and get them to add some security before we go back on air, if possible. Marty, you fly over to Fairybookville and get Mrs. Appleberry—"

"That accident-prone fairy godmother? Unh-*unh*, no thanks," Marty said. "Last time I visited her, she turned me into a purple kangaroo!"

"Exactly," Prof. Mark said. "Maybe we can get her over here to help fix Deadbeat's condition."

"Okay, boss, since you insist." Marty leaped into the air, flying over the audience through the open exit doors.

"One minute 'til air!" announced Goshzilla, eyeing the clock over the wall.

"Prof. Mark!" exclaimed an approaching human female in a park-ranger outfit. "We've got something weird going on in Jungleville."

"Park Ranger Ray-Ray!" exclaimed Prof. Mark. "What's wrong?"

"Remember that hotel project that had to be abandoned?" she inquired.

"Yeah, the construction crew kept saying something about weird voices in the basement, equipment disappearing, and refused to work until we got added security," responded Prof. Mark.

"Well, I didn't think anything about it until now, but I saw a beam exactly like the one that flooded the studio shoot out one of the windows the other night. It just missed one of our cartoon pterodactyls. At first, I thought it was the result of faulty wiring inside. That might have actually explained the weird lights. But now, all of a sudden, it just seems more relevant . . . don't you think?"

"Sure does now," agreed Prof. Mark.

"Thirty seconds to air!" announced Goshzilla. "Places, everybody!"

"Can you take Dimentrodon over there and check it out?" asked Prof. Mark.

"Good idea," said Park Ranger Ray-Ray. "He's already a puppet, at least."

"But what about *you*?" asked Thurman, his eyes getting teary. "What if that beam can not only turn cartoons into puppets, but . . . what if it comes back, and, and . . . what if it can turn *humans* into puppets, too?"

"That's what worries me," said Prof. Mark. "We've gotta fix this Halloween caper, folks, or else—"

"Ten seconds to air!" bellowed Goshzilla.

"Or else," warned Prof. Mark, completing his thought, "Cartoonyville will *never* open to the public!"

A CARTOONYVILLE COMPENDIUM (AND BEYOND):
Back-Stories from the Back Burner

I guess you could say one of my chief reasons for writing *Struggling Cartoonist* was just in case none of the following books and graphic novels ever got published, this book would carry a fairly straightforward sampler of my favorite characters from each.

I hope you enjoy reading about them.

Bigfoot Country
Deadbeat Skunk, Sezquatch, Thurman Q. Porcupine, and Girth Grizzly

As claimed in the aforementioned story, this was an attempt at a newspaper comic strip. It also might explain why I chose a skunk as one of the protagonists, since he needed to work well in black and white. The first sample week of strips showed Deadbeat Skunk and his friends consoling Sezquatch after a reporter managed to snap yet another blurry photo of him that ended up in the tabloids.

I animated a cartoon short called *Bigfoot Country: Ridin' Bearback,* and did indeed win my first Telly Award (of three) with this minute-long story where Deadbeat attempted to play cowboy with a grumpier-than-usual Girth Grizzly, who sent the skunk sailing through the clouds for his effort.

A second story carried the exhaustively long title of

Zombie Skunk Ghouls of Deadly Doom from Beyond, which was based on a screenplay written by Deadbeat Skunk. It was the story of "overnight success, which everyone wants but no one wants to admit wanting." Deadbeat found an old typewriter in his garbage-can home, and, weary of how long it takes to write a novel, decided a screenplay offered quicker-paying possibilities. Much to the dismay of his friends, a low-budget horror-movie company bought his screenplay and shot it on location in their forest.

My brother, Michael, decided to go the self-publishing route long before I did, and asked me if he did half a comic, would I do the other half? I agreed, and came up with *Comics from Concentrate*, a short-lived anthology title that, besides a handful of single-panel MarkToons gags, featured this *Zombie Skunk Ghouls* plotline. We published the first two installments, and the final installment, although scripted and fully penciled, was never inked or obviously published (self-published or otherwise). It was a shame, because I do think that story showed, just like in real life, while those closest to you may indeed get on your nerves, when it comes down to it, you show how much you really care about each other.

Doin' Time with Jayle
Jayle Bat

Jayle's actual story is the only one that blatantly contradicts her "supposed back-story" from my preceding plotline. Although I designed one somewhat cheeky spring break T-shirt, it instead involved a beach bum with binoculars hunting "beach bunnies."

Jayle came with a much more elaborate back-story. In fact, a girl like her has a rather impressive pair (of back-stories).

Jayle is sitting in her high-school study hall when she notices a hole on one side of a page in her history book. She is dismayed to turn the page over and see no hole on the other side. Turning back to the hole, she curiously scratches at it and it expands, sucking her into a time vortex that lands her in the Ice Age. (Yep, I thought of making that era into a movie long before those 3D folks. Oh, well . . . insert plaintive *sigh* here.) She helps a tribe of anthropomorphic tiger women escape from an invasion of Viking space mallards and a cybernetic rogue technician named Zebrow.

And yes, you're right, I'm thinking *exactly* what you're thinking . . .

"Too bad Roger Corman never got ahold of this idea for his first animated feature. He could have made us *both* a fortune."

I penciled, inked, and lettered the first chapter, but of course, as with all non-paying personal projects, I didn't get further than this with the panels. However, I did write and copyright a full screenplay.

There was a planned sequel based on a dream I had one night. I dreamed of a couple of people (one possibly myself) using a railroad handcart to travel through the woods on an abandoned rail line out to an old house across a dry moat.

I decided Jayle's follow-up story would be that she, along with one of the young tiger girls who decided to travel back to the present with her, would be heading back home from school (as described in the previous paragraph) the afternoon of her Ice Age adventure.

She would greet her father, a widower somewhat like Jed Clampett, and introduce him to their new intended roommate. Her father, obviously uneasy about adopting a new member to the family, has to express his objections about taking anyone else in due to a dark family secret (one even Jayle doesn't yet know about).

This idea never got further than the synopsis you've read here, except for some intriguing character sketches of rather dark minion creatures.

Petrol Jelly and the Arsonist Space Squirrels
Petrol Jelly, Krispy, and Krunchy

The scheming Krispy and his goofy friend Krunchy are a pair of city-park squirrels who encounter a talking acorn (with a derby, which I've always enjoyed drawing ever since reading *Spooky* comics, the adventures of Casper's mischievous cousin). The peach-sized acorn assures them that if they spare him instead of *eating* him, he will grant them three wishes.

Right away, Krispy exclaims that he's always wanted to be an Arsonist Space Squirrel, so the acorn grants them a spaceship and spacesuits to "zoom around the galaxy, setting fire to stuff." (Obligatory disclaimer: "Yeah, *don't* try this at home, kids!")

As they soon find Krispy's reckless steering style

sending them straight into a Steroid Belt (not a typo, folks), their second wish is for a pilot who can steer them out of trouble. Female space ranger Petrol Jelly appears and corrects their course . . . of course.

Setting the course for future stories, Petrol informs the pesky pair that she's searching the galaxy for her long-lost brother.

The Dark of NIgHTMARE
Marty the Gargoyle

As you can guess, I spent quite some time as a teenager coming up with that extensive acronym. (It stands for *Necrological Ingeniously Horrible Technology, Monstrous, And Rather Evil*. You gotta remember, Halloween has always been a thing with me.)

A trio of teenage boys lamenting their last day of summer goes to a hidden lake discovered by Marty. While sunning themselves after a swim on a small island, they discover an amulet in the shape of a basilisk (a serpentine rooster with a deadly glare), a creature coiled into a sideways ampersand. Marty gives it to his friend Mark Johnson, who draws monsters all the time.

The amulet seems to grant wishes of the dark variety, so the three of them transform themselves into monstrous "social vigilantes" to take revenge on the bullies in school.

In a way, I suppose it's very much as though *Lord of the Rings* took place in a modern high school, where the dark sorcerer is instead simply a teenager who enjoys creating monsters.

The Dark Basilisk and
Legend of the Winged Unicorn
Zhae-Garr

Just like Marty the Gargoyle claims in the story, I started writing *his* novel first, of all the characters included—at age fourteen, in fact. His original name was going to be the Gremlin, and much to my annoyance, Steven Spielberg was already producing a movie by that very same name. . . that very same year! (Oh, well. I really *did* enjoy that movie afterward.)

Also, like Marty's trio of stories, I had a tendency to keep writing my trilogies *backward*. I would hint at how they came to this point from their previous adventure, then go back and write the prequel. (Much like many *other* film trilogies today! Jeepers!)

The Dark Basilisk told of how the amulet (that Mark Johnson eventually inherited) came to be created during a pre-Columbian civilization in North America (a sort of colony of Atlantis, I suppose). After a tribe of barbarians slayed the king, to protect his daughter, Monica the court sorceress forged the amulet with the miniaturized corpse of a basilisk with ruby eyes.

To add to her challenge, the castle was being battered from outside by two warring titans: an immense dragon and a shaggy giant (one-tenth of a mile tall) named Zhae-Garr.

Monica's first act with the amulet was to curse Zhae-Garr to be weakened by sunlight, which sent him plunging deep across the ocean, back to where the only trees tall enough to protect him still stand . . . Atlantis. (Hey, I was a teenager when I wrote this, folks.)

A century or so later, in the story *Legend of the Winged Unicorn*, the Dark Basilisk amulet has fallen into the hands of a new dark sorcerer who wants to take over the kingdom (don't they always?). He creates a protective shield of storm clouds to bring Zhae-Garr back to the mainland. The sorcerer offers the permanent removal of Monica's sunlight curse in exchange for the giant's assistance in destroying the stronghold of Crystal City.

An imaginative storyteller named David Dragonscale and his centaur friend are summoned to seek the assistance of a winged unicorn in a valley far away, as a wound (even a scratch) from her horn will permanently destroy Zhae-Garr.

The Evil Plot of Dr. Ratnest
Dr. Ratnest and Daggur Bill

Dr. Victor Vincent Van Von Ratnest is fed up with his bungling minions, and gives them their marching papers. The scientist decides to create a hyperintelligent lab assistant with the aid of his Electro-Genetricide Chair. Right on cue, a pleasant-looking platypus named William Daggur, an agent from the IRS, shows up at the hilltop castle to audit Dr. Ratnest on all his lab-equipment deductions from the previous year.

Dr. Ratnest offers Daggur a tour of his basement laboratory to show him that the deductions are genuine, and suggests the agent take a seat for a demonstration.

Of course, Daggur willingly sits down in the afore-mentioned Electro-Genetricide Chair, and Ratnest prepares to flip the switch, explaining that any cosmetic alterations its subject have undergone will be mutated with horrific results.

Daggur immediately objects, as his hair plugs and dental implants will be affected—but it's too late. Metal arm and leg restraints clamp into place, trapping the platypus, who struggles helplessly to free himself.

With a blast of electricity, Daggur's teeth are warped into tusks resembling those of a saber-toothed tiger, and his hair shoots out into zig-zagging strands. Seeing his reflection and the monster he has become, Daggur Bill laughs maniacally, his crazed eyes now concentric circles of madness.

Daggur Bill goes on a crime spree collecting new equipment for Ratnest's latest evil plot, and Secret Agent Jack Anape is called on to the case.

It was much later that I realized Agent Jack Anape bore a startling resemblance to another apelike character of mine . . . Sezquatch.

Go figure.

Acknowledgments

Special thanks to my wife and daughter for their support and understanding in my various wacky projects! I love you dearly and thank God above for you both.

Additional thanks to the team at BookLogix for their assistance in bringing my first fully original fiction-book into print. Also special thanks to Gary K. Wolf, author of *Who Censored Roger Rabbit?*, for advising me to go the route of self-publishing.

About the Author

Professor Mark Stephen Smith has been teaching animation for nearly thirty years. He started with Video Animation, the very class that brought him to Auburn University Montgomery, where he got his Bachelor of Arts in Graphic Design.

In 2000, his first book was published, *The Lost World Adventures*, based on characters by Sir Arthur Conan Doyle (author of Sherlock Holmes), which Prof. Mark adapted and illustrated.

After his wife got a job offer in Atlanta, he moved to join her there, figuring it would be an opportunity to become a full-time animator at Cartoon Network. Although he tried out for a couple of shows, an hour-long tutorial on Flash (now Adobe Animate) opened his eyes to the possibilities of being a freelance animator. About this time, he began teaching at Westwood College, and started writing his second book, *The Art of Flash Animation: Creative Cartooning*.

He later joined Art Institute Atlanta, and more recently Kennesaw State and Clayton University online. He completed his Master's of Science in Information Design and Communication at SPSU, which is now Kennesaw State.

Prof. Mark lives near Atlanta with his wife, daughter, a dog, and two birds. He produces freelance animation for TV commercials, book promos, and short films, and has won three Telly Awards and an Addy for Best Sales Video.

His puppet film, *That There Hawbit: A Redneck Puppet Parody,* won a Bronze Award in the Best Parody Category of the Independent Shorts Awards, a Los Angeles Film Festival. Soon afterward, *My Sketchy Recollection* (an animated trailer for this very book) soon followed in the same film festival, this time winning a Gold Award in the Best Trailer / Teaser Category. The same film also won a Silver Award for Best Animation Short.

Prof. Mark's website is **Cartoonyville.com**.

**Other Books by
Professor Mark Stephen Smith**

*The Lost World Adventures
The Art of Flash Animation: Creative Cartooning*